Books by Best-selling Author Jerilyn Dufresne

Who Killed My Boss? (Sam Darling mystery #1)

Any Meat in That Soup? (Sam Darling mystery #2)

Can You Picture This? (Sam Darling mystery #3)

Triple Trouble (Box Set of Sam Darling mysteries 1-3)
Fall, 2014

Will You Marry Me? (Sam Darling mystery #4)

Where is Henderson? (Sam Darling mystery #5)
end of 2014

Praise for Jerilyn Dufresne and the *Sam Darling Mysteries*

Dufresne has created a charming, nosy, and slightly irreverent character in Samantha Darling, the heroine in Who Killed My Boss?, *a fast-paced cozy that takes place in the small town of Quincy, Illinois.*

Beth Amos, author of the Mattie Winston Mystery series (as Annelise Ryan)

The plot kept me guessing until nearly the end and I am looking forward to reading further adventures! Fun and entertaining read...highly recommended...well done!

Anne Kelleher, author of *A Once and Future Love* and *Wickham's Folly*

Don't miss Sam Darling's latest adventure in Jerilyn Dufresne's lively and delightful series of myseries. A great read for plane and train trips or for a week at the beach.

Mary McHugh, author of *Chorus Lines, Caviar and Corpses*, first in the Happy Hoofer series of cozy mysteries

And from Amazon reviewers:

...It's like reading the old Nancy Drew books with others. Loved it very very much!

...This book was very well written and I loved all the humor sprinkled throughout the story. Characters were loveable, not to mention the dog. Great ending.

...Sam Darling is the kind of gal you wish you could know in real life. Funny, quirky, entertaining. And her "partner," Clancy the dog, helped make this book just plain fun to read. When's the next one?!

...Very exciting plot and hard to put down. Waiting for the next book to come out. I have told all my friends about how good the book was.

...I am one who figures out the guilty party before the author does. This time I was WRONG! Very enjoyable book, fast paced...Looking forward to the next one.

WHO KILLED MY BOSS?

a Sam Darling mystery

Jerilyn Dufresne

WHO KILLED MY BOSS?

© 2014 Jerilyn Dufresne

All rights reserved.

Edition: November, 2014

Published by eFitzgerald Electronic Publishing

Cover design by Keri Knutson

eFitzgerald Publishing strives to create a professional product and a smooth reading experience for readers of indie ebooks. Please report typographical or other errors to eFitzgeraldPublishing@gmail.com.

To the eight other J's, the brothers and sisters who inspired the five Darling siblings, although the Darlings aren't nearly as sarcastic and fun as you are.

ONE

I BEAMED AS Leonard Schnitzer plucked an enameled pen from the ceramic elephant on his desk, gave it a flourish, and began to sign the personnel authorization form. I would soon be an official employee.

A scream brought us both to our feet. Schnitzer jumped up ready to investigate. I wasn't as excited as he was. Hell, this was a psychiatric clinic. People yelled in psychiatric clinics.

Before he could escape, I acted on a hunch and hollered, "Sign this first. Sign the paper." I grabbed the contract and held it under his nose, fearing that if he didn't sign it before he left the room, he never would. "Sign it," I commanded. I wanted that job. "Sign it *now.*"

Shocked, he signed.

I held on to the paper for dear life and followed Schnitzer's skinny behind right out of the room.

We joined a stampede that led to the office of my

brand new boss, Dr. Burns. A woman stood near the doorway with her back to me, papers spilled at her feet. My gaze followed hers through a maze of curious onlookers. She stared at Dr. Burns. He stared back serenely, but he wasn't seeing anything. The scene looked almost peaceful except for the blood that defaced his beautiful Persian rug.

Using offensive skills that the St. Louis Rams would envy, I pushed the group forward so I could be closer to the action. As I entered the room I clutched two strangers on either side of me when a dizzy spell unexpectedly hit. I shook it off and took a few more steps into Burns' office.

I was pretty sure Dr. Burns was dead, but then I'm a social worker and not a medical expert. Someone with a white coat and stethoscope around his neck checked Burns' pulse and stopped another man from beginning CPR, as he slowly shook his head from side to side and quietly pronounced Burns dead. White Coat must have been a doctor. But the blood on the floor told the tale, even to an amateur like me. This guy had lost a lot of the red stuff. I'd never seen this much blood in one place except at a Red Cross blood drive. He was a goner.

There goes my job.

I knew it wasn't very charitable to be concerned about my job with Dr. Burns dead on the floor, but self-preservation is a powerful motivator. I'd started my job less than fifteen minutes ago, after spending months searching for, and finally landing, a position in the private sector. Suddenly I recalled the significant piece of paper glued to my sweaty hand. A smile twitched and it was difficult to suppress it, but hallelujah—I had the contract, signed by both Burns and Schnitzer, the personnel officer. My job was secure. At least for now.

A sudden chill reminded me how serious the situation was. My shaking body convinced me I really did feel the intensity of the situation. Everyone else was shaking too—making me think we were a company full of empathy. Then I noticed that an office window was open and a freezing wind blew into Burns' death chamber. So much for empathy. No one moved to close the window.

Now that I didn't have to worry about receiving a paycheck, my concern about my erstwhile boss's death surfaced. I wondered how he died. Was it a horrible accident? Did a patient kill him? Or did he kill himself?

I surprised myself by my lack of fear, but wrote it off to being in shock. I'd probably pay for it later.

After a few moments, reason overcame my curiosity and I said, "Don't touch anything." I looked around and zeroed in on someone who didn't look panic-stricken. "Will you call the police?"

She looked down from her better-than-six-foot height, with her eyebrows raised nearly to the ceiling. "And just who might you be?"

I bit back the retort I'd been ready to shoot at her. After all she towered over me by at least a foot. "Sorry. I'm Samantha Darling and I work here. I'm a new therapist. Someone's got to call 911. Will you please call the police?" I spoke in my nicest social worker voice. Seemingly satisfied, she turned to leave.

Every person in the room seemed to flash a cell phone at me sarcastically as the guy in the white coat said, "We already called 911. Didn't you hear the yelling?"

I hadn't heard anything. But that didn't surprise me. I often tuned in to my inner voice and tuned out reality.

I turned to the rest of the curious bystanders. "Okay. Now that we know the cops and paramedics are on their way, will the rest of you please leave? We don't want to mess up the crime scene. I'll stay here and wait for the police to arrive."

My personnel office escort puffed up his chest and in a squeaky little voice tried to sound commanding as he pointed to the group with a large gesture, "Why you? Why should the rest of us leave?"

His voice barely carried over the din of the other voices, but I had no such problem. "Because my brother is a cop and I know what I'm doing. Honest, Mr. Schnitzer, I have experience with this. I'll explain it all later."

Surprisingly enough, my b.s. worked. Shock does strange things to people's behavior and they obeyed me. Mom always said that confidence is a great leadership tool.

Actually I sounded more confident than I felt. As the oldest of six kids, being bossy had become my survival skill. However, I was still nervous around a dead body. And I didn't want to tell anyone that even though I really was a cop's sister, my knowledge of crime scenes came primarily from reading psychological thrillers.

After everyone left, some of them a bit ungraciously, a mewling noise caught my attention. Lying on the floor near the door was the woman who had greeted me that morning at the reception desk. She was crumpled into an almost fetal position, crying softly, and looked nothing like the receptionist who had met me earlier. Then, her nametag had blazed proudly on her chest and the glare careening off her overly coifed helmet-head had almost matched the blinding light from her teeth. A 180-degree turnaround in less than an hour.

She was pretty in a brassy sort of way, even in her current disarray; her red-lacquered nails matched the crimson I remembered seeing on her large expressive mouth. Maybe she was younger than I was, but not by much. She looked like a person from the wrong side of town who worked hard to become someone who was no longer a social outcast.

My take was she'd never make it into the big time in Quincy, but she wouldn't get the cold shoulder in nice restaurants either.

Her voice had a slight drawl to it. The uninitiated might think she was from the south, but my bet was that she was a River Rat who crawled up to dry land. In our town in West Central Illinois, the wrong side of the tracks meant you had one foot in the Mississippi River and the other foot in mud.

Anyway, this poor wretch on the floor bore little resemblance to that perky confident employee from a scant hour ago.

The woman I'd asked to call the police returned and together we knelt to check the person on the floor. In the midst of this, we introduced ourselves, and I apologized for asking her to make a call to those already on their way. My helper was Marian Dougherty, another therapist, and a tall one at that. The woman acting as a doorstop was Gwen Schneider. We gently raised Gwen to her feet and walked her to a chair in the hallway. I asked Marian to stay with her while I checked on the crime scene.

Marian started to talk, "Why do you need to check…okay, never mind. It's because your brother's a cop and you have experience in these kind of things."

I grinned and nodded.

Her eyebrows rose again, but this time she almost smiled as I walked back into the other room.

The office was eerily silent, although the echo of Gwen's crying seemed to remain. Carefully, I closed the door behind me. I wanted quiet but didn't want to obscure any fingerprints.

Before I did anything else, I needed to stop my heart from galloping out of my chest. I closed my eyes and took a few deep breaths, practicing an abbreviated relaxation response. I pictured myself with Brad Pitt on an otherwise deserted beach. When that failed to calm me, I pictured myself alone in the same place. As my breathing slowed, so did my pulse.

Calm and thinking clearly now, I decided to look around while I was waiting for the police to arrive. Burns was lying on his back in front of his desk with his face turned toward the door. His arms were extended about shoulder level and he looked like his swan dive was aborted into a back flop. I couldn't see what caused the bleeding. It looked like it came from his neck or his head. The blood was starting to congeal in the large pool under his head, and I noticed a weird irregular blood spatter around the room. The pattern looked like a drunken circle, haphazardly touching desk, walls, carpet, and chairs. Did I only imagine the metallic smell? Suppressing the urge to touch him, I backed away. The Good Samaritan who'd checked Burns' pulse and pronounced him dead had already moved him a bit and I didn't want to add to the evidence disarray.

I observed what I could. If I were lucky, the police would ask me for information and I'd be able to supply it. My brothers were always saying I acted like I wanted to be a cop. I'd prove to them I knew how to maintain the integrity of a crime scene.

Only yesterday I had finished reading *Bipolar Passion.* The hero had managed to shoo everyone out of the murder room and kept the clues intact. The police heralded him for his astute work and he then proceeded to solve the crime. I was certain I could do the same.

I walked over to the open window, which overlooked the back yard. Wondering why it was open in January, I peered outside. There didn't appear to be anything else out of the ordinary. Except for footprints leading away from the building. In the snow, those footprints glistened. From where I was standing, they appeared to be average size. Heck, I really didn't know what I was looking for, but I thought the cops would like that I noticed some stuff. At least I'd be able to tell my brothers of my astute observation skills.

Finally, the police arrived, and when I saw the officer, I prepared for his inevitable snort.

"What in the hell are you doing here?" he asked.

"I work here; I just started this morning. Don't you remember that I came here for an interview last week? I thought you were one of the smart ones in the family."

"Damn it, Sam, you know what I mean. What are you doing in this room?" As Rob spoke, he walked slowly toward the body. It's funny how quickly a person—in this case, Dr. Burns—becomes "the body."

"I came in with a group of people after we heard a lady scream. You should be thanking me. I got everyone out and preserved the evidence."

"Are you sure you didn't touch anything?"

Typical little brother, second-guessing me. "Of course I didn't touch anything. Well, except the door, but I was careful. See, Rob, I'm looking you straight in the face. You know I can't lie when I do that."

Rob grinned and tried desperately to hide it. He was such a little cutie, almost like a kid playing cops and robbers. His dark brown hair had just a hint of red in it and it complemented the ruddiness in his cheeks.

"That won't stand up in court."

"Yeah, but it's true anyway."

A detective walked in at that moment and I knew Rob would have to turn over the investigation to him. Rob's time in the sun was over. The new arrival wore a stereotypical rumpled suit, Quincy's own Columbo. He was medium height and his salt and pepper hair barely covered his balding head. Smugly I noticed a bit of a strain where buttons joined the edges of the jacket, but had to admit he looked in pretty good shape for his age.

I knew his age—40-something, same as mine.

"Hey, Sam, long time no see. I heard you moved back to town. How are ya?"

"Fine, George. Did you notice there's a dead body in the room?" It was all right for my brother and me to be irreverent, but I wouldn't tolerate it from Butthead George Lansing, the meanest kid ever to grace the detention room of St. Francis High School. I guess I should call him "Detective Butthead." Luckily I believed in miracles, because that's the only explanation for George's success on the police force. Although he was a rotten kid, I heard he was a decent cop. He'd have to prove that before I'd believe it.

For now, I'd be cordial, but that was it.

Butthead got right down to business. "Rob, will you inform the other staff members that I want to speak to them individually, and tell them not to talk to each other about what went on."

"Sure thing."

"And send the coroner to me as soon as he arrives."

Rob nodded as he exited. I don't think George noticed Rob's quick wink to his big sister.

"So, Sam, what are you doing here? And don't say you work here, I mean what are you doing in this room?" He paused. "And why are you grinning?"

"I just noticed you called Rob by his first name. Guess you don't want to call him 'Officer Darling' in public."

"Yeah, right. So what are you doing in this room? Nosing around?" As he questioned me, he herded me into the corridor. I didn't protest. Being in the presence of a dead body was starting to get on my nerves, and I didn't want Butthead to notice.

From his questions, it looked like Butthead knew me pretty well. That was one more reason I didn't like him.

"Well, Butthea…I mean, George, I came in here with a lot of other staff when we heard a scream. One of the typists, I heard someone call her Doris, was standing in the doorway. Those files were scattered around her on the floor. As we crowded into the room we may have stepped on them. When I got inside the office I saw Burns just like you see him. Someone checked his pulse—it was a male in a white coat—and decided not to do CPR. He must be a doctor because he pronounced Burns dead. But he was the only person to touch the deceased. Gwen Schneider, the receptionist, is the woman sitting on the chair in the hall. She was crumpled on the floor in here crying. I don't think she was there when we came in, though. I kinda pushed the group forward into the room and she probably fell then. I told everyone to get lost and I maintained the integrity of the scene until Rob, I mean Officer Darling, arrived." The least I could do was treat my brother respectfully in front of Butthead.

Nearly twenty-five years after graduating from high school and my animosity toward him had not diminished. No reason to be nice to him. The jerk stood me up on prom night.

What a tool. He didn't deserve my forgiveness. Maybe someday I'd be magnanimous, but the time wasn't right for forgiveness yet. The time was right for moral superiority and looking down on him as the low-life slug that he was.

I couldn't help myself. "I know more." I kept my voice low so Gwen and Marian didn't hear.

George raised one eyebrow. "What do you mean you know more?"

"I know more but you didn't ask me the right question."

"Dammit, Sam, I didn't get a chance to ask you many questions. I asked you one and you started babbling."

I'd show him. "Okay, since you think I'm babbling, I won't tell you what else I know."

"Dammit, Sam, this isn't a game of Twenty Questions. Someone died here."

"I know. And my name is Sam, not 'Dammit, Sam.'"

He wasn't amused. "Tell me what else you think is important."

I decided to cooperate, even though he wasn't good at this question thing. "When I walked into his office for my interview last week, I heard him talking on the phone."

"And..."

"And he said something like, 'I'll have something for you next week.' And then 'Leave me alone.' I didn't think much about it at the time."

"Do you know who he was talking to?"

"Nope."

"How did he sound? Was he calm? Did he look nervous?"

I looked at Butthead a moment before I answered. "I don't really remember. What he said stuck with me because I thought it was a little unusual, but I don't think he seemed upset or anything like that."

"Okay, you can get back to work. I'll let you know when I want to talk to you. Thanks for your help in the investigation."

I wanted to wipe that stupid condescending grin off of his face. If it weren't for me, there would still be a bunch of people in the room, gawking and carrying on. Why was he treating me like excess baggage? I would not be dismissed this easily.

Not bothering to return his smile, I started to leave the room, but then had an idea.

"Hey, George, why don't you interview people in the kitchen? It's a comfortable room. When Dr. Burns gave me a tour I noticed it's isolated from the rooms where the patients will be."

"Thanks. Maybe I will."

Now it was my turn to grin. My brand new office conveniently adjoined the kitchen. I wasn't being nosy; I just wanted to help.

Okay, I was being nosy. But I still wanted to help. Maybe the cops didn't want my opinion and expertise, but darn it, I had a lot of experience with people. Plus I had my "vibes."

My brother, Rob, knew about my "vibes," but I don't think Butthead suspected. Over the years I'd begun tuning in to the strange bodily sensations I experienced sometimes. I'd get headaches or dizziness or neck spasms when I encountered something evil or maybe just weird. My body was kicking into overdrive and I knew Burns' death was not an accident or suicide. I decided to use these vibes to help me solve the murder. I figured it would be the way to keep my job. If I solved the mystery, the new boss of the psychiatric clinic would certainly reward me with job security.

In the meantime, a little eavesdropping couldn't hurt.

I'd listen a while, do some investigating on my own and then pass the information on to my brother. I was just trying to be a good citizen and to keep my job…and just possibly make Rob look smarter than Butthead.

TWO

BEFORE BUTTHEAD BEGAN interviewing staff, I decided to get settled into my office. Being next to the kitchen was a real bonus for me and my appetite. The office was full of furniture, but lacked a personal touch. I'd remedy that at the earliest opportunity. And it was small compared to Dr. Burns' mega-office, but it was cozy and it was mine.

I sat in my wonderfully overstuffed desk chair, propped up my feet on the oak desk, and looked around, giving myself a metaphorical pat on the back. Moving from government to the private sector was a bright idea.

Muffled voices from the hallway tempted me to open my door and look. Two bored-looking men wheeled Dr. Burns toward the front door. At least, I hoped it was Dr. Burns under the navy wool blanket. One death was plenty, I didn't think I could personally cope with two. I moved to my front window to continue watching as the men loaded the body into the back of the generic funeral home station wagon.

I stood there a few moments after the car left, thinking about the man who'd hired me and how quickly his life was snuffed out.

My mind wandered to my pleasant surroundings. I was happy to note there were no drapes on my windows. Long, narrow, and curved at the top, the windows were discreetly clad in cloth-covered shades that matched the appealing wallpaper.

A loveseat and matching chair, empty bookshelves, and an end table rounded out the furniture. Behind my desk was a tiny marble fireplace. Next to it sat an oak filing cabinet that I hoped to fill with case notes on exciting and curable patients.

I could live in this room. All the place needed was my stuff. I'd take care of that tomorrow. Assuming I'd still have a job tomorrow. Burns just died, but I imagined the clinic would go on functioning. At least that was my fondest hope.

Coffee, that's what I need to complete this cozy picture. Coffee. Taking one last survey of the room, I headed for the door next to the fireplace that led to the kitchen.

I found a clean mug, filled it, and returned to my office. I decided to re-arrange my furniture a bit, thinking that the desk and chair would look perfect closer to the kitchen door. My chair fit snugly in a little alcove, about three or four feet from the servants' door which led to the most important room in the house.

I settled in, deciding I needed a little quiet time, time to meditate. I wondered what Clancy would say when I told her about today's happenings.

Clancy was my best friend. And my dog. She was a cross between a yellow lab and a chow. At first glance she appeared a regular mutt, but there was much more to her than the mane-like ruff and gorgeous dark eyes. She had excellent nonverbal communication skills and our connection bordered on the psychic. I told her everything. She responded in kind.

Soon I heard voices coming from the kitchen and had no choice but to listen.

B.H.'s voice rang crystal clear as he began asking questions. I couldn't call B.H. by his given name of George, because I was still mad at him. But at least I decided to be mature and call him B.H. instead of Butthead.

My chair moved closer to the door, almost of its own volition. I smiled, thinking I had the best seat in the house.

B.H. began in his best cop manner, "Tell me what happened this morning in your own words."

An unidentified female voice answered. "I knocked on Dr. Burns' door because he told me he wanted to sign the case notes I'd been typing. When there was no answer, I decided to put the notes on his desk where he could find them later." I moved a bit closer at this point because she—I guessed it was Doris—started sniffling a little and it was hard to understand her. "Then I walked in and saw him on the floor bleeding. I screamed and I guess I dropped everything I was holding. That's all that happened until everyone else came in and then that new lady, I think her name is Pam or Sam or something, started bossing us all around and made us leave."

It's really amazing to me how some people can misinterpret someone else's decisive actions as bossiness. Well, obviously, Miss Doris had some unresolved authority issues that she needed to deal with. But unless I wanted to be accused of bossiness again, I probably wouldn't tell her about it.

B.H. continued, "Did you hear anything this morning that sounded suspicious or unusual?"

"Uh-uh." Which I presumed meant "no."

"Has there been anything else going on that was unusual?"

"No, not really (sniff, sniff). But that new guy in town that started the private investigating agency—what's his name...Mick or Mike or something?"

"Michael O'Dear?"

"Yeah, I guess that's his name. Anyway, he was here this morning and saw Dr. Burns, but I don't know why."

It's unfortunate that vibes don't travel through walls and doors. I couldn't get a feel on whether she knew anything else or not. And who was this O'Dear guy? A private detective in Quincy? I wondered why he visited Burns this morning. Was it detective work or a psychiatric visit?

B.H. continued with the questions, "How long have you worked here? Did you get along with Dr. Burns? What time did you arrive this morning? Describe what you did from the moment you arrived until you found Dr. Burns. Did Dr. Burns have any enemies that you know of?"

What I got from the answers was that Dr. Burns wasn't in the running for Nice Guy of the Year Award. I overheard "crabby," "aloof," "overbearing," and "distracted." I was almost glad I hadn't gotten to know him.

Too bad B.H. didn't need my help in the room. Maybe he wouldn't notice if I went in and made a fresh pot of coffee.

He did notice. With the same stupid grin on his face, he stopped the conversation until I made the coffee, waited for it to finish brewing, poured myself a cup, and walked out of the kitchen. A full ten minutes. He was good.

B.H. repeated the same conversation with other staff

members, but elicited no new information. Several of them remarked on my ability to take charge of a situation. Perhaps they phrased it a bit differently. I recall hearing the word "bossy" a few times, but resolved that I wouldn't be bothered by the remark. People just needed to get to know me a bit. They'd come around. Listening to them was getting to be boring; the same information was repeated time and again. I was patient however, and soon my persistence paid off. Miss Gwen Schneider arrived for her interview.

By this time, my ear was firmly implanted in the door.

"Miss Schneider, can you tell me what happened this morning in your own words?"

"Boo-hoo, sob, sob, slobber, snort."

The interpretation being, "I know plenty, Bub, but I'm too broken up right now to talk about it."

Through the wall I couldn't get a feel for whether she was upset because she loved him or because she killed him. Or maybe something in between. And I didn't know whether to feel compassion for her or antipathy. Or maybe something in between.

Despite her slobbery sobs, I heard her say that when she walked into Burns' office with the rest of us, she was overcome with grief. She said she fell to the floor and didn't recall anything else until "that bossy lady told Marian to take me into the hallway."

Decisive. Decisive.

It looked like it was time for another cup of coffee.

Without glancing at B.H., I slowly ambled to the coffeepot. When Gwen continued crying, I put my mug on the counter, walked to her, and placed my hands on her shoulders. Looking in her eyes, I asked if I could help. She shook her head, but absolute misery just poured off of her. She was in so much pain. At that point it didn't matter to me whether she'd killed him or not, she was really suffering. I let my hands slide around her and hugged her to me. She resisted for a brief second and then literally collapsed onto me. Her sobs shook her body for several minutes. I was very focused on her and didn't notice until later that B.H. kept silent and didn't interrupt.

When she started to regain her composure, B.H. looked at me and mouthed "Take her out of here." I was glad to oblige and it wasn't entirely done out of the goodness of my heart. This seemed like a good opportunity to tune in to her, ask some questions, and see what was going on.

We left the kitchen and went into my office. I guided Gwen to the loveseat and sat beside her. For a while she continued to sniff and cry into a tissue I'd given her, and then looked at me suspiciously.

"What do you want?"

"Nothing really. I saw that you were hurting and wanted to help."

She half-smiled. "I'm surprised."

"Well, I am a social worker. It's kind of built in."

She started snorting and sniffling again. "I don't deserve your sympathy. I don't deserve anything but jail. I didn't mean to, but…" the snorting sound effects continued.

Aha, here was my chance. "You didn't mean to what, Gwen?"

Before she could regain her composure to answer me, I suddenly felt someone was in the room with us. I repeated my prompting, "You didn't mean to what, Gwen?"

Too late. She'd controlled her blubbering and wasn't going to give me anything.

The feeling that someone was with us remained.

My footsteps were slow and quiet as I inched toward the kitchen door. I recognized the same heavy breathing on the other side that I remembered from the back seat of a '65 Chevy during high school. With a jerk I pulled the door inward, and just like in a Charlie Chaplin movie, in fell B.H. himself. When I saw him lying there, it did wonders to temporarily appease the revenge mentality I felt. However, he didn't even have the good sense to look embarrassed.

"Miss Schneider, I'd like you to accompany me to the police station. We need to talk some more." He stood as if nothing had happened.

Guiltily and hastily, I blurted, "Gwen, I promise I didn't know he was there. Besides, I know you didn't kill Dr. Burns."

"But..."

"It doesn't matter how I know, I just know." There's no way in the world I could try to explain to this grieving woman and Detective Butthead that Gwen didn't "feel" guilty. "Get yourself a good lawyer, and I'll stay in touch."

"Now, Miss Schneider, there's no need to get a lawyer. I just want to ask you a few more questions down at the station. You are not being accused of anything and you are not under arrest." Butthead did the best he could to intimidate me. He glared.

I glared back. He was a rank amateur. As the oldest of six kids I had the "sister look" down pat. I could silence a mortal at thirty paces. He pretended it didn't bother him, but he didn't fool me. I knew he was cowed.

As they left, I resolved to find out everything I could about this case. Gwen obviously knew more about the murder and certainly felt guilty about something, but I knew she wasn't the killer. So my quest was to find the one who did the deed.

I felt up to it. The odds were that no one would fire me or lay me off until well after the funeral when the business affairs were settled. Until then, no one would realize that I didn't have any work to do.

Heck, half the office probably didn't even know I was hired. Still, I'd heard that Dr. Burns liked to assign patients to new staff members himself, so I didn't have to worry about being asked to do any actual work for at least a few days. I thought I could earn my salary by looking for who killed the boss. Maybe people would be so impressed that I could keep the job. Who knows? But as my son would say, "Yeah, and maybe pigs will fly out of my butt."

On that note, I set to work. At least I thought about setting to work. It was quitting time.

My first day on the job was certainly eventful. My main concern now was to solve this case, prove to be indispensable and keep my job.

THREE

"NO, NO, PAOLO. I can't stay with you. I belong to the world."

"Cara mia, stay. I will treat you like the queen that you are. The world will survive without you, but I will not." He began kissing my fingers and slowly and deliciously moved up my arm until he got tantalizingly close to my open lips.

I was torn between pretending hesitancy and following my heart…and my body.

Brrng, brrng.

Shoot!" The phone jolted me awake, and I was not in a good mood. Giving up Paolo wasn't fun; he was the best dream man in a long time. Before I picked up the phone I glanced at the sturdy athletic watch on my wrist. *Six A.M.?*

"Yeah." It wasn't my most clever opening line, but it would have to do.

"Sam, this is Jenny. We got a problem in the ER and need a counselor. I see that you're on call. Rise and shine."

"Is this your idea of a joke? I just got hired yesterday. Couldn't be on call yet."

"Get in here, sis. We need you. You know I wouldn't lie to you. The on-call sheet says you are the designated hitter, so come on."

"Yeah sure." Clever retort. When it came to my younger sister, I was always quick with the witty dialogue. "Okay. What do you need?"

Jen was actually Jennifer Darling Vu, Director of Emergency Services at Bay General, the local hospital, and married to Dr. Manh Vu, a pediatrician, originally from Vietnam. We were happy to have him in the family for a lot of reasons, not the least of which was that he provided free pediatric care to the growing family.

Being the oldest of six was both a gift and a curse. I loved the gang and their assorted spouses, significant others, and kids. I also resented the fact that I'd had to get a divorce in order to have a bedroom to myself.

Jen interrupted my ruminations. "We have an ER full of drunks and I think we need a crisis intervention specialist, rather than calling the police. Can you come in and help?"

"Sure, be there in a few minutes." As I hung up, I actually felt pretty good. Jen asked me for help very infrequently and I was glad to oblige. Before I had applied at the clinic, Jen told me that Doctor Burns negotiated a nice little contractual relationship with the hospital, so that the psychiatric division of the clinic provided emergency crisis intervention and therapeutic intervention on an as-needed basis. The on-call therapist did the initial assessment and determined if the psychiatrist needed to be called. Illinois was one of the states where licensed clinical social workers were allowed to practice independently and even receive insurance payments.

I dressed in jeans, T-shirt and wool sweater. Quincy was cold in January, especially this early. I put on boots and a parka, grabbed my phone and keys and started to leave. It felt odd that there was no one to tell that I was going out. My divorce was a thing of the past, but I was used to having my children around. Their departure was too recent for my solitude to be very comfortable. Adam was a junior at the University of Illinois, and Sarah was in her first year at the same school. After the holidays, they had both gone back to school early because of their commitments, and, I suspected, because of their respective love interests.

As I left, I made sure the answering machine was plugged in. Then I realized I did have someone to notify. Clancy had been following me around ever since the phone rang. She had been sleeping on my bed, and when the phone rang she raised her regal head and gave me her "get off your butt" look.

I crouched down to her level. "I need to go to the ER. I promise I'll be back in time for your morning run. And remind me to tell you about my dream. It was a corker."

I could tell from the doubt in her eyes that she didn't believe we'd still do the run and consequently felt neglected, but I didn't have time to deal with her hurt feelings. The drunks needed me.

As I left my home, the porch light went on in my landlord's house.

"Darn it." I tried to hurry to the garage door, hoping to avoid being spotted by the bane of my existence.

"Sam, oh Sam. What in the world are you doing leaving home at this time of the morning? Surely your new job does not require these hours?"

There she was. Loud, flower-endowed housecoat. Bright pink curlers surrounded by a garish scarf. Eyes squinting in spite of her glasses. Nose sniffing the air, trying to smell God-knows-what. My landlady. My nemesis. My Georgianne Granville.

This is not the neighborhood of my youth. I grew up about six blocks away in a decent working class neighborhood. We always walked by the "rich" section wondering what the lives of the inhabitants were like. Since my recent return, I now knew how the inhabitants lived, because I was one of them. Well, sort of. I rented one of the carriage houses in the ritzy section. It was nice, cozy, and had a great mailing address. I rented from the eccentric Georgianne Granville, one of the "grande dames" of the town. She was in her 80's now but was still a frequent subject of the society pages in the local paper. I wondered how her husband, Gus, tolerated sharing the same house with her.

"No, Georgianne, these are not my normal working hours. I just got a call from the ER and I need to hurry. Sorry I don't have time to chat." *Exit, Sam. Now. Hurry.*

"But, Sam…"

"Bye-bye. Say 'hi' to Gus for me, will you?"

A narrow escape. Getting ambushed by Georgianne sometimes meant hours of entanglement, but I've improved in doing the "Ditch Georgianne Dance" in the short time I've been back in Quincy.

One of the benefits of living in a small city is that it doesn't take much more than 15 minutes to drive anywhere. I walked into the ER less than 20 minutes after I was abruptly awakened.

I hurried to the triage area, where patients were being evaluated as to the severity of their needs. There is usually an air of excitement in the ER and my adrenaline always starts flowing when I arrive. I've been in emergency rooms many times, sometimes to meet Jen for lunch, sometimes when my children or I needed emergency help, or many times in Chicago because of my job with the Department of Children and Family Services. When a child was injured because of abuse and neglect, one of my duties was to meet them and the family at the emergency room and make some immediate decisions as to the placement of the child and siblings.

I waited while a secretary fetched Jen. As I looked around the ER, I thought of the many reasons I had decided to return to Quincy and change jobs. During my interview, when Dr. Burns asked me why I left DCFS after fifteen years, I found it hard to answer.

I didn't know which answer to give him. The one that said I'd been imagining the pleasures of working with people with short term neuroses—people who had hope for the future? Having worked for DCFS in Chicago, I was a bit discouraged about my inability to make a difference in people's lives. Should I have told him that I finally completed my master's degree and returned to my hometown ready to change jobs?

What would he have thought if I had told him that there were times when I was almost convinced I had actually helped some folks, but that was the exception, not the rule? Or if I'd mentioned how many midnight calls I'd made to homes where kids were screaming, parents were screaming, neighbors were screaming, and I was screaming? Taking kids away from their parents, even for one night, was one of the worst jobs imaginable. Far worse, however, was interviewing families after a child had been killed through abuse or neglect.

Should I have told him I wanted to change jobs because I didn't think it was a sin to want an easier job and make good money?

Why then did I feel guilty about this career change? It wasn't like I was selling out or anything. I wanted to work with people with insurance. No big deal.

And I wanted to stop dreaming about those kids.

The noises of the emergency department brought me back to the present.

So much for my fantasy of dealing with patients in a nicely appointed, clinical office. I was hired yesterday and here I was…in the ER again.

I wondered why the Clinic hadn't notified me that I was on-call. I remembered Marian Dougherty mentioning that she was the on-call therapist for the week. Resolving to clear that up later, I found my sister holding emesis basins for two different patients. She handed one to me, said something about making myself useful, and began filling me in.

I couldn't pay attention to what I was doing. Watching someone vomit is not my idea of a good time. Instead, I looked at my sister. Jenny was a year younger than I and ten years more mature. She was short, blonde, and thin, and managed to look good in the ugly green scrubs. If I didn't love her I would have hated her.

Most of my sibs were in helping professions, with the majority in the medical field. I was a notable exception to the medical sibs, based primarily on my inability to deal with anything coming out of any orifices of the body. Consequently, it was difficult for me to listen to Jenny. The gagging noises I made drowned out much of the conversation. I was able to gather that there were fourteen patients who were not only inebriated but had probably gotten into some rotten homemade elderberry wine and most of them were violently ill. I still didn't know why she needed my help as the patients seemed much too busy throwing up to be causing any major problems. Finally, Jen asked me to step into one of the treatment rooms with her. Handing the emesis basin to a grinning EMT, I followed her into Treatment Room #3. I began to get a bit suspicious as Jen lagged behind me and pushed me into the room ahead of her.

"Surprise." "Congratulations." "Welcome aboard." My eyes could barely see everyone, because of the tears that suddenly spilled onto my cheeks. There was Ed, Pete, Jill, and Rob. With Jen behind me, the whole family crew was there.

"I can't believe you guys set me up like this. It's so

early in the morning that it's practically the middle of the night."

Jen moved into the center of the crowd. "It's the only time we could get everyone together."

It was a wonderful surprise and I continued to grin as I looked around at them. Most of us looked alike and were obviously siblings.

Jenny was around five feet tall, with short no-nonsense dark blonde hair. Ed was tall and rangy. He had remained a towhead, and his hair kept falling into his eyes, just as it had when he was a kid. The tallest of the six, Pete had wheat-colored hair that curled in waves around his ears. Those curls had always made me jealous when we were younger. Jill wore her ash blonde hair in a ponytail today. Most of the time she wore her long hair up on top of her head, in a misguided attempt to look older. Rob was the only non-blond. His dark brown hair shone with a hint of red in it.

And wonder of wonders—everyone was getting along. This was one for the record books.

Most of the gang worked at that very hospital, which we affectionately dubbed "Darling Memorial." Mom and Dad had figured that we owned most of it anyway since all of us were born there.

Jen quickly poured the punch, cut the cake, and then cut out of there to get back to work. With a breezy, "Love you," she headed back to the inebriated masses. I visited with the rest of the crew until we heard a scream coming from the waiting area. Wondering if this was the continuation of my surprise party, I led the sibs out to see what was going on.

We came upon a scene straight from "COPS." A young man paced in the waiting room, holding a gun and waving it haphazardly—now at the ceiling, now at frantic bystanders.

"This damn place don't care about people. All they care about is money. Nobody here gives a damn. We ought to close it down. Everybody get out; don't give them no more money." He started weaving as he gestured. "What happened to Dr. Burns is gonna happen to a lot more doctors around here."

Ed, Rob and I all made a move to deal with the situation. I guess it really was Ed's place as Director of Hospital Security. But Rob was a cop and was technically on duty all the time. I was going to intervene because I was pretty good at crisis intervention, and since I was fairly codependent I was always eager to help.

The three of us were doing our variation of a Three Stooges routine when a man walked into the waiting room, calmly approached the dude, did a modified karate chop to the wrist and grabbed the gun before it hit the floor.

I was impressed. I was more than impressed; I was staring. The hero was a giant, muscled god. Every wannabe surfer girl's dream.

Rob identified himself as an off duty cop and took over. As he held onto the miscreant he turned and said, "We're going to need a statement from you, Mr.—uh I didn't catch your name."

"O'Dear. Michael O'Dear."

Aha. The private eye who visited Burns yesterday morning.

O'Dear glanced around the room, his eyes finally lighting on me. I managed to fluff my hair and wet my lips before I realized what I was doing.

I smiled and stuttered, "Sam Darling."

His smile drew me a step closer. "My name's Michael, but you can call me 'darling' if you want." He handed me a business card.

"No, my name is Sam Darling." Why couldn't I wipe the idiotic grin off my face?

I tore my gaze away from him and decided to do my bit to help. I started to gather the witnesses in order to interview them.

"Sam, if you want to be a cop, why don't you be one?" Ed said. "And if you don't want to be a cop, then let us handle it. I'll take care of the details here. Go home and get some rest."

I agreed but without much spirit. It's really hard to be the bossy older sister when your brothers keep insisting on taking over.

I discreetly turned my eyes to O'Dear and found that he was still looking at me. My mirror often lied to me and told me I didn't look my age and that my smile and eyes were gorgeous. I didn't believe my mirror. However the way the god looked at me made me think he believed it.

Oh, God, please let him be single. Please let him be straight. Please let him like me. Please let him carry me off to his villa in Spain. Oh, God, please let him...

His smile broadened. His easy confidence when he winked and grinned made me feel like a country bumpkin. As he walked away, his smile seemed to linger. Not in a Cheshire Cat kind of way, but in a Prince Charming kind of way. I imagined him climbing into a chariot with a surfboard attached and heading for the nearest beach. That would be Hogback Island in Quincy Bay, which diminished the romance of my fantasy.

He intrigued me. Then I glanced at his business card and was reminded of his name.

Yeah right. We'll fall in love, get married, and my name will be Sam Darling O'Dear. Not on your life.

"Hi ya, Sam."

Just my luck. Why would B.H. be the cop to show up?

Doesn't he ever go home?

I greeted him. It wasn't a frosty greeting; after all, Michael was still within hearing distance and I wanted to make a good impression on him. At the sound of the detective's voice, Michael walked back to our area.

"Michael, this is B.H. Lansing, a detective with Quincy Police Department. B.H., this is Michael O'Dear."

B.H. shot a confused look at me as he shook Michael's hand. "The name's George Lansing."

I shrugged as they talked for a few minutes, mostly about Burns' murder. B.H. ended their short conversation with, "I understand you were meeting with Doctor Burns shortly before he died. I'd like to speak to you about that later this morning."

They agreed on a meeting time and place, then B.H. wandered off, following Rob and the guy who provided such cheap entertainment for the ER.

My curiosity, as usual, got the better of me. "I do have a question before you leave." Michael arched his eyebrows and nodded. "What are you doing in the emergency room this early in the morning?"

Chuckling, he said, "I was about to ask you the same question. Maybe we could get together some time and talk about it."

"Okay." The stupid grin on my face was probably

going to stay there for a long time. I tried to get rid of it, but no such luck. I was stuck with it.

I couldn't help but think that the guy who stood me up just met the guy who's gonna take me out. There's a certain symmetry to that.

FOUR

WHEN I GOT home from the hospital there wasn't time to do the things I'd planned: take a leisurely shower, eat breakfast, and pick up my junk scattered around the house. Those chores could wait. There was one task I couldn't put off. The first thing I saw when I walked in the door was Clancy, standing by the couch with her leash in her mouth, holding me to my part of the bargain. When the kids and I brought her home as a puppy, she promised to be faithful, protect us, be there when we were lonely, and in general, just be cool. In return I promised to walk her and feed her, things she reminded me to do on a daily basis.

The morning walk was always a special time for me. Clancy knew where we were going and led the way to the park down the street. I didn't have to think about any of the details. She stopped at every street corner and looked both ways and then pulled me across when it was safe.

The scenery along the route was beautiful. Much of this neighborhood was on the National Historic Register and rightly so. Today Clancy and I walked by the Clinic. At this time of day it really looked like the mansion that it was. Built by one of the trade barons in 1880 when most of the town was making money hand over fist, it was one of the masterpieces on this street. The builder of the mansion, Jeremiah Woodson, one of the founding fathers of Quincy, started out in poverty, but through judicious use of a boat he owned, eventually parlayed a small nest egg into a remarkable fortune. In those days, there were many like him, and most of them built their homes on Maine Street and those surrounding it. The Clinic was the diamond among many jewels.

I was fortunate that I lived on such a street and that I had Clancy as a tour guide.

When I first saw Clancy at the Humane Society, I felt her sadness in a physical way. I found it hard to explain, but her pain was palpable. She was lonely and she was scared. I chose her immediately, with no objection from my kids.

Since the moment Clancy came into our lives, she has been my closest confidante. She understands me better than anyone else in my life. She also accepts none of my b.s.

I didn't fear the snow and ice because Clancy took care of the mechanics of the walk. All I had to do was go along. This was my thinking time. I solved many of the world's problems during these morning walks. Too bad I wasn't so successful in solving my own problems. They weren't monumental, but they were constant. Clancy's heard them all. "You know, Clancy, social workers don't earn huge salaries, but things are really looking up now that I'm at the clinic. And the cost of living is a lot less here in Quincy than it was in Chicago. I think things will improve in the money department. Maybe I'll be able to buy you the gourmet dog food." Clancy responded positively to that idea; her tail went crazy. I wished all of my problems could be solved so easily.

My other problem was a lousy love life. Lousy? It was nonexistent. I'd been divorced from Alan for several years, and had had a few dates, none very serious. Clancy stopped and looked at me. "Okay, Clancy, I didn't realize I said that out loud. One of these days I'll find Mr. Right. Heaven knows I've been successful at finding Mr. Wrong. Maybe I'll just reverse my tactics. That ought to work. Yeah, I know I'm just talking; this is Fantasy Island. Right?" I felt embarrassed verbalizing this stuff. I was a feminist before the word was invented, but when I fantasize, there is always a Mr. Right. This morning he looked alarmingly like Mr. O'Dear.

During this walk, however, my thoughts drifted mostly toward THE MURDER. In my mind, it was always capitalized. THE MURDER. My first. I was intrigued.

"I know I should be sadder about Burns' death. I'm a social worker. I almost feel guilty that I don't feel bad enough. I didn't know him though, and when I met him last week for my interview there was something about him that gave me the creeps. Even though he was smart enough to hire me, I couldn't make myself like him."

We crossed a busy street. It only momentarily stopped my babbling.

"Well, I don't know why I didn't like him, but his eyes were cold. When he noticed me staring, they got warm again. It was weird. So I'm sad that a human being is dead, but I feel no real loss of Dr. Burns. Does that make sense?"

Clancy nodded, then headed back to her job of leading the trek.

There was one good thing about this murder investigation. It would take my mind off the empty nest at my house. "God, I miss the kids. They're growing up so fast and pretty soon they'll be gone for good, instead of just away at school." Clancy looked at me with empathy. I stooped and patted her as I continued, "Well, I'll never really be alone. I've got you and the rest of the clan. Even though I live by myself…" A low growl emanated from Clancy, "Oh, sorry, girl. Even though you and I live by ourselves, we're never really alone. Relatives are always stopping by, and we get invited over to their homes a lot. Moving back here was definitely the right thing to do."

I'd missed the support of the family over the years, especially when Alan left me. I loved Chicago, but Quincy was still home. Besides the sibs and their spouses and kids, there were myriad aunts, uncles, and cousins. Sometimes they got on my nerves, but it was neat to be a member of this club. Even though the membership list was so long it appeared that anyone could be a member.

I also told Clancy about the "John Doe" from the ER. "What do you think is going on with him? What possible reason could he have had for threatening people like that? Did I tell you that he said other doctors might die like Burns?" She pondered that one for a bit. "Why am I so worried about him? It's not like I'll ever see him again."

Clancy gave me her "hey, stupid" look.

"Okay, he did threaten other doctors. Maybe I will see him again. Wonder if he had anything to do with Burns' death?"

Her eyebrows raised as she thought about that notion.

"Nah, Clance, he didn't feel guilty to me. He just felt ill. There's a difference."

And why did Michael O'Dear's face keep popping up in my mind? The last question I didn't verbalize. I didn't want Clancy to hear me thinking so much about a man; she might lose respect for me.

I chuckled as I realized that all of these questions made my life sound like a commercial for a soap opera. But, anyway, I found myself looking forward to seeing O'Dear again a lot more than I wanted to admit. Clancy scooted out of my way as I tripped on a curb. I caught myself before I landed face down in the snow. "Guess I'm a little preoccupied."

I swear she chuckled.

We finished our walk at a brisk pace. After returning home, I got Clancy her food and water, showered and got ready for my first real day in the office. I didn't have much time to learn about my job or do any work yesterday since Dr. Burns' murder overshadowed my appearance as the new kid on the block. I'd spent most of yesterday sitting in my new office with my ear to the door.

Today I would settle in. I filled my briefcase with framed pictures of the kids, my license to practice as a clinical social worker in the state of Illinois, and a small plaque painted by a friend that said, "God has entrusted us to each other." Those would fill my desk until I messed it up with files and books.

I also put a few boxes of books by the front door, ready to go into my car. Those would fit nicely into the built-in bookcases in my office. I was excited about going to work, although I was bummed about my boss being dead. Since I had a choice, I decided to go with the excitement rather than dwell on the sad stuff.

Everything was ready but my all-important outfit. After I poured a cup of coffee, I wandered into my walk-in closet. Actually, it was a climb-in closet. It was piled almost to the ceiling with "stuff," things I'd been promising myself I'd put away as soon as I had time. I moved aside the Scrabble game and old Rolling Stone magazines and took out my good suit. It had seen me through a lot of tough times, but I wore it the other day for my interview. Would the other staff members recognize it? Would it matter if they did? Didn't I have anything better to obsess about?

I wore the suit.

I said good-bye to Clancy and left home feeling a bit ambivalent. On one hand, I had optimism and hope in my heart for my newly organized future. On the other hand, I was saddened about Burns' demise. It was difficult sorting out the emotions.

Because of all my paraphernalia I decided to drive to work again. The trip was a short one, and I arrived around seven, a full hour before I was required to be there. I describe myself as an on-time employee. My family would call it compulsive behavior.

Schnitzer hadn't given me a key yet, but I had a feeling Gwen Schneider would be there early and would let me in.

The first part was correct anyway. She was at her desk. I peered through the glass door, like a little kid waiting for the toy store to open. I rapped gently at first, but finally ended up pounding with both fists when I got no response to my polite approach. Somehow I knew she heard me. Even through the glass, I could sense her nasty attitude toward me. I couldn't figure out why she disliked me already. When I came for my interview and was a visitor, she treated me like royalty. And yesterday, after Burns' murder, she even allowed me to comfort her. Normally people had to work with me a few days before they didn't like me.

Could she be jealous of me? Nah, it must be something else. Maybe she was embarrassed that I saw her at her worst in Burns' office. She was the first person I could accurately describe as a blithering idiot. Not a professional description, but accurate all the same. I was going to find out what was going on with her. In the meantime, I would dazzle her with kindness—and maybe b.s. She wouldn't be able to stand it.

She finally deigned to acknowledge my existence. As she walked slowly and deliberately toward the door, her hips swayed as if she meant business, but her hair didn't move at all. She'd cornered the market on hair spray. When she opened the door, she flashed her pearly whites and said, "Good morning. Were you waiting long?"

"Yeah, I was." I thought lying was a waste of time, and besides I wasn't very good at it. "Why wouldn't you let me in?"

"I didn't hear you." She apparently thought that she was good at lying. Her eyes betrayed her. "Would you like some coffee?" Her smile didn't falter, but the rest of her body language gave a little bit, and her eyes were glistening as if she'd been crying. She turned to the coffeepot behind her desk. My vibes must have been taking a break, because I didn't get any strong emotions emanating from her other than sadness. Why wouldn't she let me in if she was just sad?

I decided to be noble and forgiving. She had a hard time making eye contact, but I didn't. I walked around her desk and touched her on the shoulder. "Gwen, I know that Dr. Burns' death was hard on you. I also know you probably spent most of the night at the police station getting grilled. Whatever is going on with you, I am not your enemy. I know you didn't kill him and I'm willing to help you."

She nodded and started sobbing. She ran toward the bathroom. I started to follow her, but figured I'd done enough damage already.

I picked up the coffee that Gwen had poured for me and I meandered to my office. Meander is the correct word because I took a few wrong turns. The scenic route. Instead of turning left from the waiting area, I accidentally went right and then left and I walked past a conference room and several smaller offices. When I reached the back of the mansion, I continued left, making a circle through the building. This route took me past Dr. Burns' office.

I fought the urge to look around the crime scene.

After Burns' office came the kitchen, then my office. My very own office. I didn't share it with anyone. That was so cool.

I put down my briefcase and purse, went back out to my car two more times for the boxes of books, and finally did a very important, symbolic act. I rummaged through my briefcase full of stuff and poured the coffee from the clinic mug into my own mug. My sibs gave the mug to me on the occasion of my employment by DCFS. It said, "Just take it one, gigantic, earth-shattering crisis at a time." The cup appeals to my smart alec side and survived fifteen years with the Department. It remained my talisman.

Throughout the morning people kept poking their heads into my office and welcoming me. As expected, the big topic of conversation was the murder. Everyone had a favorite villain. It made for pretty interesting conversation, and I didn't have anything better to do. I probably would have a few days of light duty before I got some patients assigned to me.

Besides trying to catch all the available gossip, I used this time to study policies and procedures. I really wanted to learn the important things about the company—like how many vacation days I got per year, how much sick time, personal days, all of the vital stuff.

I wondered when B.H. would be back to question the rest of the staff. Marian Dougherty came by my office and asked me to join everyone in the kitchen, which doubled as the staff lounge. She introduced me to others I hadn't met. In this office, most staff members were counselors, social workers, and psychologists. There were also a few nursing personnel. Most of my co-workers seemed friendly enough, and since I took charge yesterday, they all continued to ask me questions. I pretended I knew a lot more than I did.

I used all my knowledge garnered from *Bipolar Passion* and *Schizoid Revenge*, my latest forays into reading psychological thrillers. Although my favorite books dealt primarily with the mental illness angle of murders, they also had incredible details about crime scenes and police procedures. Everyone seemed impressed with my knowledge, and I hoped that changed their minds about my bossy demeanor yesterday.

When Gwen Schneider entered the room, a chill

entered with her. Earlier Marian told me Gwen worked for Dr. Burns for almost the entire time he was in practice. I knew there was more to her than met the eye, but vowed to let it drop. Or at least I vowed to try to let it drop. Being nosy is a genetic disorder I inherited from my mother. There is no cure.

I tried to observe my surroundings instead of staring at Gwen. This kitchen was huge. Most of the appliances were ultra modern but were in muted tones that blended in well with the Victorian surroundings. We all sat around a butcher-block table that was large enough to seat my whole family. I wondered idly how they moved it to clean. Three of the walls were covered in a yellow washed paper. The fourth wall was natural red brick. Homey and inviting.

No matter how I tried not to look, my glance kept moving to Gwen when I thought no one would notice. She was antsy, unable to sit still, but I didn't feel the same amount of animosity as earlier. Her energy was really disorganized. Almost chaotic. Even though I noticed things like this, I didn't know what to make of it. My gut told me that Gwen Schneider was in major hot water. Or maybe not. Maybe she was mentally ill. There I went again. I decided to go with my feelings that she was in big trouble. Of course, anybody who knew she spent last night being questioned by the cops would know she was in trouble. *Nothing like going for the obvious, Sam.*

FIVE

OKAY, PERHAPS I'M not the most tactful individual, and grace is not my strong suit, but you'd think I'd be able to ask people questions without them thinking I'm trying to dig up some dirt. Apparently not.

So, armed with good intentions and gut instinct, I began my quest for the villain. I decided to hang out in the kitchen because sooner or later everyone passed through there. Also it was close to the scene of the crime, and I knew that curiosity would get the better of everyone eventually. They would all feel the need to get close to where it happened. Burns' office itself was taped off with the yellow pre-printed crime scene tape. For some reason, that surprised me. I almost expected generic masking tape, on which someone might have written, "Do not enter. Crime scene." I guessed the QPD had more professionalism than I thought.

Even so, murders were rare, and part of the reason I moved home. The last murder I recalled happened when I was a teenager. "Old Lady" Tippins beat the hell out of

"Old Man" Tippins one too many times and he died. Immediately upon being notified of his death, she also died. Which just goes to show you that love comes in a lot of varieties, and there is no age limit to the *Romeo and Juliet* theme.

I sat in the kitchen waiting for the unsuspecting staff members to wander in. The first one was Marian Dougherty. She gave me a sideways glance as if she knew I was going to fire some questions at her. Discretion would be my watchword.

"How's it going, Marian?"

"Uh, okay." She fiddled with the faux pearls around her neck, eyes darting everywhere but in my direction. She seemed like a nice enough person, and had sincerely welcomed my arrival. I'd heard Marian was a decent therapist and a genuinely caring individual. She was about my age, a bit overweight, with reddish sun streaks in her almost black hair.

"Is your work going well?"

Her reticence vanished. It was as if she was ready to talk and I was the lucky person who happened to be there at the time the dam burst.

She sighed and said that it was hard doing therapy when her mind was elsewhere. She asked if I thought we could legitimately cancel appointments because of Dr. Burns' death.

"Who's in charge of the therapists?"

"No one now. Dr. Burns supervised all of us directly and there's not a middle manager on the behavioral health side."

She and I both came to the same conclusion. We would suggest to the rest of the therapists that they evaluate all of their patients and cancel the appointments they thought were appropriate. There might be a few people with problems so acute that it would not be in the patients' best interests to cancel. We figured that whoever was in charge of the clinic would surely close the whole office for Dr. Burns' funeral and appointments could be shuffled if necessary for that occasion. Today was Thursday and the funeral would probably be Saturday or Monday, depending on the wishes of the family. We'd probably find out more about that tomorrow.

So, now that she was trusting, I got to the meat of the discussion. As she innocently poured a cup of coffee, I pounced.

"So, this was really a surprise, huh?"

"You think people get murdered in Quincy every day or something? Of course it was a surprise. Dr. Burns was a dear man." Marian added teaspoon after teaspoon of sugar to her coffee. "Well, maybe not a dear man, but a good man. Well…"

I got the picture. And filed it away in my brain for

later retrieval.

She continued. "Anyway, my paycheck never bounced. He sure knew how to run a business. I'm going to miss him. At least I'll miss him sometimes." She stirred her coffee without looking at it, unaware that the hot liquid sloshed over the sides of the mug. "Well, to be honest, he could be a real jerk, but no one should have killed him. Nobody deserves that. I always thought there was more to Gwen than met the eye, but I didn't think she would kill him."

Whoa, the verdict was in, even before Gwen had been arraigned. She hadn't even been arrested. In fact, she was still sitting in the reception area, trying to muddle through.

The joys of small town living. Probably everyone in town was by now debating her innocence or guilt. Since people love a good scandal, the majority was probably convinced of her guilt.

I decided to probe a little more.

"What makes you think Gwen killed him? Had there been trouble before or something?"

She hesitated and looked around before answering. "You know they were having an affair. And I'm not one to gossip, but Gwen never married and she worked late a lot and Dr. Burns worked late a lot and Gwen always has expensive jewelry and her mother stopped talking to her and she never goes to the Christmas party because Mrs. Burns will be there, and…" At this point she stopped to take a breath and I was glad. I had begun worrying that she would keel over, her face was so red. I started talking before she could go again.

"That's very interesting," *and juicy,* "but if they were having an affair, why would Gwen kill him? That's kind of like biting the hand that feeds you." I was quick with the clichés.

"I don't know why she would kill him, but I heard she confessed right in your office." *Damn those heating grates.*

"She did not confess. Please tell everyone that. And I don't think she killed him. I can't reveal my source right now, but I trust the truth will become evident to everyone very soon. In fact, a trusted investigator is on the case even as we speak." It wasn't my fault that Marian probably assumed that the trusted investigator was Michael O'Dear instead of me.

Thinking of his name reminded me that I was eager to see him again. Maybe I could weasel some information out of him, but I had to have a plan. For now I had a witness to milk for information. Maybe I mixed my metaphors a little, but I was getting excited. And that feeling was one I hadn't experienced in quite a while.

I continued, "I only knew him a few minutes before he died, so I didn't form an opinion of him."

Marian raised her eyebrows in disbelief.

"Okay, so maybe I have an opinion, but I want to hear more of yours. What did you mean, 'he could be a real jerk sometimes'?"

Marian hesitated. "I probably shouldn't be telling you this, but he wasn't a very good psychiatrist. Great businessman, poor therapist. Over the years I've taken several of his former patients—after all there's not another clinic for them to go to—and they're almost pathetically grateful that I listen to them. Apparently, Dr. Burns was pretty directive. I've even heard him described as manipulative."

I certainly didn't get this personality profile in the few moments I'd known him. This was some good stuff. I tried for more but Marian was finished with her sharing.

She left the kitchen soon afterward when she realized that I was not going to say anything interesting. I waited for the next victim.

Soon Doris walked in, took one look at me and walked out. I felt pretty put out about it, but figured that Marian must have passed the word about my prowess as an interrogator.

There weren't any evil vibes surrounding anyone in the office, so I decided to take my quest elsewhere. First, I called one of my favorite human confidants to see if he was available for consultation.

He picked up the phone immediately. The sound of his voice always made me smile.

"Pete, Sam."

"Hi, Sam, what's up? Something important to talk about?" No beating around the bush with Pete. He cut right to the chase. I think he's the only other one of the siblings who was psychic too, but it's not something we talked about. I just know that Pete and I have always used shorthand language with each other. We finished thoughts and sentences and sometimes the others felt left out. Of course, like any dysfunctional family, we all finished sentences for each other and talked over each other, but this was different. It was special.

Pete was the head nurse on the cardiac care unit at the hospital. Like me, he had recently returned to Quincy. For a number of years he served as both a priest and a nurse at a mission in Maui. We teased him that being stationed on Maui was kind of defeating the purpose of making the sacrifice to be a missionary. We didn't tease him too much though, because all of us were able to take a cheap vacation at one time or another, courtesy of Father Brother—Pete's nickname. For reasons known only to Pete, God, and me, he was on sabbatical and had come home for a while. And he was extremely successful at the job he chose. He had a special compassion for people that was beautiful and rare. He was indeed a great gift to all of us. Of course, we wouldn't be caught dead saying that to his face.

"Yeah, it is important. Are you free? Can we get together?"

We made arrangements to meet in a half hour at The Dairy, a favorite family gathering place. The location was ideal, as it was between our family home, the church, and elementary school. Besides, it had a table big enough to accommodate all of us.

I arrived twenty-five minutes later and met Pete as he was walking in the door. After a quick hug, we moved to our favorite table even though there were only two of us today.

Pete's Irish cable-knit sweater, worn over a green turtleneck, complemented his curly blonde hair. He had a great profile too; one of the few who didn't inherit the family pug nose. Females in town called him "Father What-a-Waste."

Marge, the waitress, nodded and we knew she'd bring over two black cows—the Midwest equivalent of a root beer float.

"What's up?" he asked. As usual, Pete didn't waste time.

I really loved this man. When he was born, he'd already had a glow about him that had not diminished. As a five-year-old I had remarked upon the glow. Well-meaning aunts quizzed me about it. They thought I was either hallucinating or having religious visions, neither of which was acceptable in their view. They would have preferred the religious visions, but even that would have raised eyebrows. So I stopped remarking on the things I saw and felt. Mom and Dad knew, or suspected. I think Mom may have had a bit of the "feeling" herself. Or at least I like to think she did.

"I need to talk over some things. My boss was murdered yesterday." I waited for an exclamation of surprise and was disappointed when it didn't appear. I had forgotten that the murder had happened over twenty-four hours ago. I hadn't seen a newspaper or listened to the news. Surely people as far away as Marblehead, a distance of six miles, knew and also probably knew who did it. Well, doggone it. I didn't know who did it. And I wanted to prove everyone else wrong.

"Gwen didn't do it, Pete."

"If you say so, Gwen didn't do it. Now let's talk about who might have killed your boss."

And we set to work.

SIX

PETE AND I talked for a long time, but we didn't come up with any likely suspects. I knew it was time to stop when we started giggling over probable candidates like the butler, the upstairs maid, our sister Jill, Butthead, and Dr. Burns himself. We said goodbye and made plans to get together soon to continue the discussion. I knew I could count on Pete to keep things hush-hush. I certainly didn't want Ed and Rob to find out I was working on the case. And, above all, B.H. could not know. My greatest thrill would be to solve the case, give some credit to my brother, Rob, and leave B.H. in the dust.

My hostility toward B.H. was probably juvenile, and I even felt guilty about it, but I wasn't ready to give it up. He'd broken my heart.

I arrived home a few moments later to an angry dog. Over my profuse apologies, she got her leash and then waited impatiently for me to check my messages before we left for the walk. I had one message. From Michael O'Dear, asking if I'd go out to dinner with him on

Friday. I couldn't wipe the smile off my face. At the end of his message he asked if I had heard that Gwen Schneider had killed Dr. Burns. He sounded smug. But he didn't have the knowledge I had. I knew she didn't do it. I knew it for a fact, beyond a shadow of a doubt. Of course I had no proof, but I wasn't going to let a small thing like that stand in my way. I just needed to find the killer.

I called Michael's number immediately, told his machine that Friday would be fine, and that I'd be ready at seven. It was hard sounding sophisticated while doing a happy dance around my living room.

I smiled at Clancy as I tried to make up with her. She is my significant other and I couldn't afford to have her mad at me. She finally gave me one of her "okay, you're only human" looks and handed her leash to me. I accepted it gratefully and we headed for the park.

This part of the city had a lot of parks. In fact, many of the lawns were large enough to qualify as well. I put myself on automatic pilot and concentrated on the case. I had never met Mrs. Burns but planned to see her at the funeral home. Other staff told me she was a nice lady, but they said it in a way that seemed they didn't quite mean it. I also heard she was a beauty and quite a bit younger than the doctor. I was anxious to meet the woman who had been married to the enigmatic Dr. Burns.

Clancy and I walked for over an hour and both of us got nice and sweaty. That felt great while the blood was still pumping, but it soon chilled me to the bone. I wanted to hurry into the carriage house, but saw Mrs. Granville's curtains move as I started to pass.

"Clancy, she saw us. Act sick, so I have an excuse not to talk long." Clancy immediately obliged and hung her head as she stuck out her tongue.

"Oh, Ms. Darling, may I speak to you a minute?"

Smiling my phoniest smile, I approached her verandah. Other people would have called it a porch, but to Mrs. Granville it was, and would always be, a verandah.

Georgianne Granville had on her usual evening attire: a quilted bathrobe, pink fuzzy slippers, and pink plastic curlers that were covered by a diaphanous scarf-like apparatus. With all her money, I wondered why she didn't have better taste in at-home loungewear. She pulled herself up to her full 4'10" and spoke to me as if she were Queen Elizabeth II on her balcony.

"Ms. Darling, I saw a man looking around the carriage house today while you were gone. I hope you don't plan to have people lollygagging around while you are engaged elsewhere."

"No, Georgianne. My plans don't include the lollygagging of people around my house. Did you see what he looked like?"

"Well, I wasn't really looking." She couldn't see me roll my eyes in the dark. "But he appeared about twenty-five to twenty-eight, dark hair, a little shaggy around the ears, he had on a brown corduroy jacket with the patches on the elbows. So outré, don't you think? And he was looking very suspicious. But as I said, I really didn't get a good look."

That didn't describe any of my brothers, Michael O'Dear, or B.H. Lansing. Aha, as they say, the plot thickens.

"Well thanks for telling me. By the way, how is Gus today?"

"He is still very ill and unable to have visitors."

Just then a booming voice echoed out of the open door, "Sam, is that you? Come in here and see me, girl."

Ignoring Georgianne's grimace of distaste, Clancy and I both bounded up the stairs and into what Georgianne called the parlor. Lying on the couch was one of the nicest men ever to grace this earth. Unfortunately, he probably wasn't going to be gracing it much longer. I thought he would probably live a long and healthy life if it weren't for his wife. But maybe that's too cruel. Some people enjoy sparring with their partner, it keeps them lively. I know I enjoyed it too, until I discovered that my husband was sparring with someone else at the same time. Sparring outside of marriage was against my personal belief system.

What Georgianne knew and didn't like was that I had known Gus for many years, ever since I was in elementary school. I had been brave enough to not only walk past the rich people's houses, but also to dawdle a bit. One day, I came upon a gardener, working in a flowerbed at the Granville's. He was singing WWI and WWII era songs in a booming baritone. I joined in. He was surprised that someone my age would know these songs. I later told him how my mom had taught me songs from her youth and from her own mother's youth.

I began helping Gus the gardener nearly every day after school and he taught me many more songs. It was fun singing and playing in the dirt. I'd run home right after school and change into my blue jeans. Gus always wore overalls. In the summer he wore an undershirt and the other seasons he wore comfortable old flannel shirts. I began asking him questions about the rich people who lived there. He told me that money wasn't everything. And I said I wouldn't know, never having had any. So he started paying me a quarter every time I helped. Eventually he revealed himself to me as Gus Granville, the owner of the home. Well, actually he said his wife owned it and she let him live there. With that, he laughed the loudest, most beautiful laugh I'd ever heard. He laughed until he cried. I did too, although I didn't know what I was laughing at.

I kept in touch with Gus over the years, stopping by whenever I was in Quincy. He cherished pictures of my kids, attended their baptisms, and grieved with me over the death of my parents. He grieved again with me when my husband left. Other than my family and Clancy, Gus was the best friend I'd ever had. When I returned to Quincy, I bunked with Jen and her brood for a few weeks while I looked around for a place to rent. When Gus found out I was looking, his eyes twinkled and he said he had just the place for me. He put on his overcoat and boots and took me out back to the carriage house. Like a proud artist, he pointed at it, wanting me to love it as he did.

"Don't tell the Missus I told you this, but we've had a few spats over the years. When we were young I decided I didn't want to get mad and leave, but I needed a space to call my own. So I converted the carriage house into an apartment. Lately, I haven't felt the need or the energy to use it, so it's empty and would be perfect for you. Please take it."

I said "yes" without even looking at it. Knowing it would bring such joy to Gus and such agony to Georgianne were enough reasons for me. When I went inside, I knew my instincts were correct. There was a small kitchen downstairs, with a nice sized living room, small dining room, and large master bedroom and bath. Upstairs were two small bedrooms and another bath. It was just what I wanted and needed. There was room for the kids when they came home from school, but my personal living space was all on one floor. I moved in the next day, converting the dining room into my office. My brothers and sisters were huffing and puffing, but we got the job done. I was very happy in my new home and even happier with one half of my landlord couple.

When I tuned back in to the conversation, Georgianne sniffed her distaste and continued a diatribe already in progress, "…I insist. Please take your animal outside and tie it up. We cannot have animal dander in the house. My husband is ill and his breathing will be compromised. Surely you don't want to be responsible…"

Gus interrupted, "Leave the girl alone, Georgie. Go ahead, Sam, tell me what's up."

Georgie? I managed to avoid a fit of the giggles and went on. "It was really something. No sooner had I started my new job, than Dr. Burns was killed. I was still in the personnel office filling out forms when I heard the scream."

Gus responded that he'd heard details from his neighbors already. "I probably knew almost as soon as you did," he chuckled.

I asked him if he had known Dr. Burns well.

Gus sat up so I could join him on the couch. "I wouldn't say I knew him well. I did know him for a lot of years. Hell, this is a small community and we lived in the same general neighborhood."

"Did you like him?"

Gus laughed again. "I didn't care much for the old fart," he became serious, "but I'm sorry he was killed."

"Please don't use such vulgarities." Georgianne reminded us she was still around. "I'm sure you can convey your meaning in a more refined manner."

"Sure, honey." Gus said to his wife, and then turned toward me again, "I didn't care much for the old bastard, but I'm sorry he was killed."

He cocked his head to look at his wife, "Is that better?"

That did it. The laugh that I'd been able to suppress finally forcibly exploded. "'Scuse me."

Gus smiled and Georgianne pouted. I liked that.

I asked Gus if I could bounce some ideas off him. He brightened up.

"Sure. I'm bored stiff cooped up in this house all the time."

"Okay, here's what I want to know. Even though you don't get out much I know people visit you all the time.

So do you know if anyone hated Dr. Burns?"

Gus laughed. "If anyone hated him? It'd be easier to list the people who didn't hate him. There weren't many of those."

"Well, he did give me the creeps. But why did everyone dislike him?"

"I dunno. He seemed to have everything but always wanted more. Then when his wife started making so much money, I think he got a little jealous."

"Wait a minute. What did his wife do to earn a lot of money?"

"Guess you haven't heard about it since you've been gone so long, but Carolyn Burns is actually Felicia Greene."

"Whoa. Burns' wife is Felicia Greene? I don't believe it. I've read all her books."

"Yep. She's quite a bit younger than Burns and rumor has it that she got bored one day and just started writing. Surprised everyone when she got published. Burns didn't fuss too much about what he called 'her little hobby,' as long as it didn't infringe on his life. His only input was to insist that she use a nom de plume so no one would know his wife was a novelist."

"This is unbelievable. Her books are my favorites. I mean they have everything in them—murder, sex, intrigue, mental illness. She's got the workings of the mind down pat. Was she involved in the mental health field too?"

Gus chuckled before he spoke. "I don't think Carolyn Burns worked a day in her life before she began writing. Wait until you meet her and then tell me what you think."

I pictured Mrs. Burns as middle aged and dumpy and thought she must have used someone else for the author's picture on her book jackets. After all, Dr. Burns was in his sixties and the young woman pictured as Felicia Greene certainly couldn't have been married to him. I'd heard Burns' wife was younger than he was, but there were limits to my imagination.

"Ms. Darling," Georgianne again, "my husband needs his rest. I think it's time for you to be going."

"Sure thing, Georgie," I loved calling this formal, cold woman by her nickname.

As I kissed Gus on the cheek he said "No need to rush off," but his tired eyes belied his words.

"I've got a lot to do. I'll see you soon though."

Gus replied, "I think I'll feel well enough to attend the funeral. It's likely to be a real shindig and I don't want to miss it. I'll see you there."

Clancy and I entered our home just as the phone was ringing. When I answered it, two youthful voices said, "Hi, Ma." It was Adam and Sarah calling from school. I'd called and told them about my boss's death and they wanted to know how I was holding up.

"I'm fine. I'm sure sorry he was killed. It was really a bad experience for everyone, and I imagine his wife is devastated. I haven't paid my condolence call yet, but I'll meet her soon."

"Mom, you seem way too excited. What else is going on?" Sarah knew me too well.

"Well, I just thought I'd look around a bit and see if I can help your Uncle Rob solve the case." Surely my kids couldn't object to that.

"Mom," Adam's turn, "remember, you're a social worker and not a cop. Leave the detective work to Uncle Rob and his coworkers. Stay out of it. We don't want anything to happen to you."

When did my lovely son turn into a man? "Listen, you guys, I'm fine. I'm not doing anything stupid and I can take care of myself. Remember who the parent is here. Now, be good little kids and get back to your homework."

We spoke for a few more minutes and after I hung up the phone, I kept thinking about them. It hadn't been easy after the divorce, but all in all the kids turned out fine. I was so proud of both of them. I also loved the fact that they were at the same school, and was grateful that they had each other while they were gone.

I made dinner for Clancy and me. In the past I had been a firm believer that dogs should only get dog food, but ever since Clancy and I have been alone, I've changed my mind. Many times, she and I have shared the same meal. I'm a vegetarian however, and Clancy didn't used to be, but she's almost converted; she does have her limits and draws the line at tofu. I warmed up leftover vegetable lasagna and put some in her bowl along with some canine morsels. I poured myself a glass of Sauvignon Blanc and sighed contentedly. Sometimes life was really good.

I had just finished my meal and was making a pot of decaf, when I heard a light tapping on my door. I opened it without looking to see who it was. Another bad habit from my childhood, but it's one I had a hard time breaking. It took a moment for my eyes to adjust to the darkness; then I noticed a man standing there. He was hiding in the shadows, and rocking back and forth on his heels.

I said, "Can I help you?"

A sad voice asked, "Are you the new lady at the clinic?"

I answered in the affirmative.

"Are you Father Brother's sister?"

Again I answered affirmatively, and then added, "Well, I used to be; I mean he used to be. Well, yeah."

"I know him from the hospital and he told me about

you. I need to talk to you. Can I come in? Please?"

The "please" did it. I didn't know too many bad guys who would look and sound so sad and who would say "please" when they wanted to enter a house. So I stepped aside for him to enter. Besides, Clancy was still eating—a sure sign the stranger posed no threat to me.

As he walked into the living room, I thought he might be the person that Georgianne Granville described. When he stepped into the light I also noticed that he was the "John Doe" from the ER earlier in the day.

The first thing I said was, "Tell me your name." I was tired of this "John Doe" thing.

He looked surprised at my directness, but answered, "Charlie Schneider."

The puzzle pieces were multiplying, but a few were starting to fit. "Any relation to Gwen Schneider?"

"Yeah," he said, "she's my sister. That's why I'm here."

"Well, I thought it also could have something to do with the incident this morning in the ER. I saw your fascinating performance and since I'm a therapist and occasionally accept private patients, I thought you might be here for some counseling."

He gave me a look he could have learned from B.H. or Clancy. I decided to mind my manners and not glare back. Clancy didn't have any such reservations, however. She decided to acknowledge his existence by staring.

Charlie didn't notice.

"Can I sit down? I'm kinda tired."

I offered him a seat and I joined my dog on the couch. "Why don't you just tell me what I can do for you?"

He glanced around a little before looking me straight in the eye, and said, "They arrested my sister tonight for murdering Dr. Burns, and I know she didn't do it. She told me you said you would help. Since you're Father Brother's sister, I thought I could trust you. I don't know who else to go to, so here I am."

He made perfect sense to me, and that was scary. I quickly reassured him, "I know she didn't do it, Charlie, but I don't have any proof."

"I'm your proof," he blurted. "I did it."

The corpse was barely cold and I'd already solved the murder. God, I'm good. Even Clancy was wagging her tail.

SEVEN

SO I WAS sitting in my living room with my dog and a confessed murderer. And what did I do?

"Charlie, would you like cream in your coffee? How about another piece of pie? You look like you could use something more to eat."

I wouldn't let him talk while he was finishing the leftover lasagna, garlic bread, and pie. This was every mother's dream—someone who really appreciated a good meal. I didn't think it necessary to tell Charlie that the lasagna was made by Mama Manicotti in a sterilized kitchen and that the pie was frozen before I popped it in my oven. He gulped down two cups of coffee as if he were freezing. As he let out a very satisfied belch and wiped his mouth with his sleeve, I realized this guy was probably not the brightest porch light on the block. I also knew he was innocent. My vibes were dormant; there were no errant physical sensations. And it made me mad that he felt he had to confess. This guy was as innocent of murdering Dr. Burns as I was. It was obvious that he was trying to protect his older sister, Gwen.

I decided to try to get a little more information. "Charlie, will you tell me what was going on with you in the ER this morning?"

He looked sheepish; his unstructured hair fell into his eyes, a shield protecting him from the world. "Yeah, they make me so mad in them damn hospitals. My wife and little baby was hurt bad a couple years back in a car wreck and we didn't have no insurance and they took 'em to the hospital and they both died there." Charlie had a hard time maintaining eye contact; his eyes darted back and forth from the plate to Clancy, scarcely alighting on me. "They're still sendin' me bills. It's like they don't know there's human beings on the receivin' end of them bills. Every time I get one of 'em, I get a little crazy. But Dr. Burns said I wasn't crazy. He called it something else, like post dramatic stress."

More information. Charlie was seeing Dr. Burns professionally and was diagnosed with Post-Traumatic Stress Disorder. He would be a perfect candidate for the villain. PTSD, mood swings, the victim was screwing his sister—literally, and the hospital was screwing him—figuratively. Too bad he wasn't guilty.

"Charlie, will you answer another question for me?"

He nodded.

"Did you get arrested this morning for what you did

at the hospital?"

"Yes, ma'am, I did. But they know'd me down at the police station and they let me out until the court day. My lawyer said it'd be awhile. Heck, I'll be in jail anyway for murder, so this thing won't count for much extra."

"Why are you saying you killed Dr. Burns, when I know you didn't?"

"I did too kill him."

"Okay, why did you do it?"

"Just cause I wanted to, that's why."

"So you killed him because you wanted to. How did you do it, Charlie? What did you do to him?"

He stuttered a bit, unable to come up with a plausible method. I was convinced that neither of us knew how Burns had been killed, but I knew more about it than Charlie did. I'd seen Burns dead.

"Sorry, that's not good enough. I know positively that you are innocent. Unfortunately, I can't reveal my source at this time." I was getting tired of saying that. "What's going on?"

"Well, they got my sister and she didn't do it neither. I thought 'cause I'm such a screw-up anyway and I don't have nobody but her, that I oughta say I did it. That way she'd get out."

"Don't worry, Charlie, she'll get out anyway. I'm going to help her by finding the real killer. Now the best thing for you to do is to take good care of yourself and make sure you visit her a lot."

He nodded. After crossing our fingers for luck, and pinky swearing that we wouldn't tell anyone else about me working on the case except Pete, otherwise known as Father Brother, we parted company for the night.

I felt absolutely drained, but I also felt such an adrenaline rush, it was hard to settle down. "Clancy, how about an extra outing tonight? I feel like running a little."

She returned with her leash even before I finished my sentence. I put on my boots and parka and we started out. The snowy night was so bright that I could see clearly. The ground was already covered and flakes were once again falling. I couldn't run much because of my boots and because of the snow, but I knew I had to try, or I'd never be able to sleep.

We started jogging around the big house, but then hit a patch of ice. Clancy skidded; I let go of her leash and windmilled my arms trying to avoid the inevitable. No such luck. With a giant thud I fell flat on my butt. Luckily I had enough padding so I suffered no injury. And because there were no witnesses other than Clancy, even my dignity wasn't damaged. I laughed so hard that I couldn't get up. Clancy was laughing too. We couldn't stop. The guffaws were flying from both of us. The Granville's light went on and I knew that Georgianne would soon be on the back porch with a shotgun, looking for the intruder. I still couldn't get up, so I belly crawled next to her house so she wouldn't be able to see me. Breathing heavily, I pulled Clancy close and begged her not to make any noise.

Sure enough, "Who is it? I've called the police. You better get out of here."

I could just picture her hair in curlers and a gun in her hand. Gus, long weary of his wife's eccentricities, would be snoring happily upstairs. After a few moments, she went inside and I was able to limp back to my house, dragging an unwilling Clancy with me.

"I know I lied, Clance, but my energy is gone now and I can't run. Besides, I'm literally freezing my butt off. Would you like some hot tea and cookies?"

The bribe worked. We drank. Then we slept.

An early phone call the next morning from Schnitzer in the personnel department notified me that the office would be closed until after Dr. Burns' funeral on Monday, so I had the whole day to myself. I could clean house, solve the murder, or think about going out with Michael. I chose Door #2 and decided to do some sleuthing.

First things first. I called Angie, my brother Ed's wife.

"Darlings." She loved to answer the phone that way.

"Angie, hi, this is Sam."

"Oh, hey, I heard about the tragedy at your office. So sorry about it. And to think the murderer was right under your nose. She worked for him for almost twenty years, I heard."

"Yeah, yeah, yeah, but that's not why I called. I want to make a call on Mrs. Burns and I either need to pick up a dish from the deli or call upon my favorite sister-in-law to see if you have anything freshly baked just laying around."

I could hear the grin in her voice. My family was used to covering for me at potluck dinners and carry-ins. "I'm your only sister-in-law, and it just so happens I've made two bundt cakes. And you can have one. Good timing, sis." Angie was an only child and has certainly adapted well to the vagaries of a big family. She knew how to go with the flow.

"Thanks, Ang, I'll pick it up in a little while. I owe you." I couldn't begin to count the number of times she rescued me. God help me if she ever decided to keep track.

"I know you do. Can you babysit for Skeeter tonight so we can go to the game?" There was no need to tell me which game. St. Francis University had a superb basketball team and the entire town attended the games.

"Love to but I can't. I think I have a date. Don't laugh. I really do. But next time you need a sitter, you got one. See you in a few minutes."

After hanging up the phone and also saying good-bye to Clancy, I stopped to speak to Gus for a while. I'd seen Georgianne leave a few minutes earlier.

"Hi ya, gal." Gus was genuinely glad to see me.

"I want to run a few things by you." He nodded and put on his "business" face.

"Right after we discovered Burns' body, I saw his receptionist sitting in the corner of his office, sobbing. A little while later she said, 'I didn't mean to do it, but…' and then she started sobbing again. It sounds like she was trying to confess, but I don't think she did it. The next day she acted really weird when I arrived at the clinic. Pretended she didn't hear me knocking, and then acted phony-sweet to me. I can't say I like her, but I'm convinced of her innocence."

Gus didn't bother asking me how I knew Gwen was innocent. "Maybe she's just in shock. Finding Burns dead like that would be enough to make anyone act a bit goofy. Why don't you give her a few days and see how she behaves?"

"And I'm the one who's the therapist? You're right. Her behavior is consistent with people who suffered a traumatic event."

I thanked him, gave him a peck on the cheek, and made my getaway before Georgianne's return.

I drove the few miles to Ed and Angie's. As I pulled into the driveway, I couldn't help but smile. The lawn could not be described as "neatly manicured." In the past it had been littered with bikes of various makes, colors and sizes. Now most of the kids were older and drove cars, but the yard still held reminders that a large family lived there.

Ed and Angie had committed the big "no-no" and so they got married immediately after graduating from high school. Alice was born a few months afterward, then Susan, John, Robert, and fourteen years later the ever popular Skeeter.

Skeeter met me at the door. He was dressed in bib overalls and a long sleeved T-shirt. Perched on his head was his favorite baseball cap that said, "Cute." He was cute; in fact he was downright adorable. He was adept at walking; and he smiled and drooled at the sight of his Aunt Sam. We had a great rapport, and spoke each other's language. Even though I was in a hurry, I couldn't resist crawling around on the floor with Skeeter for a few minutes.

As someone with a "favorite Aunt" status, I always bought kids toys that I liked. That way I had something fun to play with when I visited them. So Skeeter and I played with a talking truck for a short time.

Angie hollered from the kitchen, "Sure you don't want

to stay for lunch? Ed'll be home in a little while."

"I'd love to, but I can't. Gotta visit Mrs. Burns." I grabbed the cake, hugged and thanked Angie, scooped up Skeeter, and promised to spend more time with him as soon as I could.

Then I drove back to "my" section of town. The Burns' home was a conglomeration of styles, a white quasi-Spanish-Moorish-Victorian-Tudor-Queen Anne home. It was built in 1887 and was one of the showplaces of Quincy. It was a favorite in the annual "let's show off our homes" tour. I'd never been inside, and was kind of looking forward to it, wondering how anyone could live in such a hodgepodge house.

I rang the bell and tidied myself up a little, brushing off stray Clancy hairs from my coat. A stiff looking guy in a black suit with tails opened the door. It couldn't have been a butler, but it was. A bit pretentious, even for this section of town. I swear he would drown if it started raining, his nose was so far in the air.

He said, "May I help you?" and I introduced myself as an employee of Dr. Burns. It didn't seem important that I tell him the employment was for less than an hour prior to Burns' death. Anyway, he let me in and took my coat. As he opened the closet, it was apparent that my coat, like me, didn't quite fit in. Choosing to ignore this, I followed the sound of voices.

The room I entered must have been the drawing room. It was too overdone to be called a living room, or even worse—a family room. It was enormous, but it was hard to tell a lot of the details, because it was literally brimming full of people. I looked around for Mrs. Burns. Although we'd never met, I recalled seeing her name in the society pages along with Georgianne's. The only photographs I'd seen were the ones that appeared on the back covers of her novels, but I didn't believe those pictures, which showed her as young, brunette and pretty.

I saw a few people that I recognized from the neighborhood, and grinned when I noticed Gus sitting on a sofa, holding court. He had always been a popular guy, and was even more so, now that he no longer got around much. Georgianne always discouraged visitors, but they kept coming anyway. Once you knew Gus, you found it hard to stay away for too long.

I placed my cake on a table in the hall. Joining Gus on the couch, I took advantage of the momentary lull in his entourage.

"Hi. You feeling better?"

"Of course, Sam. I always feel great when I see you."

My blush lit up my face like a neon sign. *I wish I took compliments better.*

"What's everyone doing here? In my family, we have

the wake the day of the funeral. Why are they holding the party of the century before the funeral, with Burns hardly cold?"

Gus smiled, "I think everyone is a little curious. Murder and mystery are scarce in Quincy. No one wants to miss out on anything." At that he glanced around to see if his wife was nearby. "Including Georgianne. I must admit it didn't take much convincing to get me to come. I'm curious too. Not much excitement in my life. Thought this might be interesting."

I hugged him and stood. "Well, I need to express my condolences. Can you point out Mrs. Burns to me, please?"

As he pointed, I gasped. There, talking to my future date, was one of the most gorgeous women I had ever seen. Much more beautiful in person than in pictures. At the same time, a wave of revulsion washed over me, unlike anything I'd ever experienced. Even if I wanted to second-guess my ability, I couldn't at that point. I was literally doubled over with psychic, painful vibes. The woman made me sick.

Michael rushed over and Mrs. Burns arrived at the same time. They both grabbed me. And I fainted. Yes, I swooned. Not only was I in the presence of all of the money in the city, but this was the first time Michael had touched me—and I passed out. I wouldn't know what class was if it bit me in the butt.

Michael and Mrs. Burns helped me into an adjoining room. With my keen observation skills, I guessed it was the library. Hundreds of books lined the walls. I reclined on a chaise lounge, and Mrs. Burns immediately placed a cover over and around me, probably not from any sense of care, but because she didn't know what to expect from me next, or maybe so I wouldn't touch her fancy-schmancy furniture.

I tried to be gracious. "Thank you very much, but I'm fine now. I am so sorry, Mrs. Burns." It was hard to be nice when this woman made me dizzy and sick to my stomach. I'd never had such a powerful negative reaction to a person before. If this was what tuning into my psychic abilities would do, then I thought I'd pass.

Normally I'd just get a crick in my neck or a dizzy, light-headed sensation. This was an entirely too drastic reaction. The only possible explanation was that Mrs. Burns must be the murderer.

"No need to be sorry, dear." Dear, indeed, and this from a woman who either was twenty years younger than me or else had extensive work done on her face and body. I hoped it was the latter. There must be something in the rulebook that states a widow cannot look so sexy at her husband's wake. At least there has to be a paragraph somewhere that says they can't wear skintight black wool crepe dresses. Especially in front of my soon-to-be date. She continued to be solicitous, "Are you sure you feel well? Is there anything I can get for you? There are a few doctors in the other room. Would you like me to find one for you?"

After saying, "No thanks," I reclined and panicked. Panicked and reclined. The panic subsided somewhat, but the reclining didn't. Now that I was more accustomed to being in the presence of a murderess, I was feeling better physically, but still couldn't figure out what to do. I needed to get rid of her so I could talk to Michael.

"I'm sorry to bother you, but could you please get me a club soda?"

She didn't look like she wanted to leave me alone with Michael. Maybe she had designs on him. God knows, he was good looking. But he was mine. Or soon would be, as soon as I sat up and started charming him.

Anyway, ever the dutiful hostess, Mrs. Burns slithered out of the library.

I shot into an upright position. "Michael, she did it!"

"No, she didn't, Sam. All she did was touch you. You passed out. It wasn't her fault."

"No, I don't mean that," trying hard to sound competent, "I mean she killed her husband."

Did he have a glint of amusement in his eyes? Or was

it a patronizing look one gives a child? Or maybe, he just felt a little woozy himself because of my mesmerizing effect on him.

"What makes you think she killed her husband?" The detective in him couldn't resist asking questions.

With that he put his hands on my shoulders and gently pushed me back into a reclining position. He stroked my hair and I melted. Again. Tingles everywhere. And a dangerous remnant of dizziness.

"Well, I can't really tell you my source. Just trust me. I know it and I'm not wrong. Believe me, Michael, I'm not making this up. Please…"

My pathetic whining must have done the trick. Michael took my hand, looked into my eyes and said, "God, you look horrible."

Then he smiled, and I couldn't be mad at him. "Yeah, I know I look bad, I just fainted; but that doesn't change the fact that Mrs. Burns killed her husband."

"Carolyn didn't kill anyone, Sam." Carolyn? Since when was my soon-to-be-beloved on a first name basis with a murderer?

"Michael, she did, and I'll prove it." At that, Mrs. Carolyn Burns returned with my club soda and smiled at us. Actually she was probably smiling at Michael. See that's what makes me mad about cute guys. He didn't do anything wrong and already I'm mad at him. Haven't even had our first date and I'm jealous. That really steams me. Why did he smile back at her? Does he always smile so broadly at murderers or just beautiful women? Or was he just covering so she wouldn't suspect that I suspected? Just being in the same room with her was getting to me.

"Thanks, Mrs. Burns, but I need to go home. There's a bundt cake on the hall table. That's for you. Gotta go. I'll be back for the funeral Monday. Bye. Oh, I meant to tell you I really like your books."

With that I tried to get up. I looked at the smiling Mrs. Burns and felt dizzy. As I stumbled against Michael, Mrs. Burns put out her hand and touched me and I—omigod, not again—the room started spinning and soon I did too. The last thing I saw was a delicate Asian vase on an end table. It got closer and closer to me as I fainted. Her eardrum-bursting shriek brought little satisfaction but it did rouse me from my faint. She must have thought I was going to break a precious possession in this pristine palace. Michael apologized to her, said he would see that I got home, and waltzed me out the door. As soon as we were away from her I immediately felt a little better, but I didn't look better.

"Come on, let's get you home."

Embarrassed, I said, "I feel fine now, I promise. I can make it home. Besides, you're all dressed up, so you probably need to go home and change into comfortable clothes before you pick me up for dinner."

"Dinner? Sam, you must be kidding. You just fainted. Twice." He paused. "Are you sure?" I didn't think I liked the amused tone, but I was willing to overlook it for now. Besides I was too embarrassed to say very much.

"I promise I'm fine." I looked him in the eyes so he would know I was telling the truth. Then I remembered, he didn't know that about me. In fact he didn't know much about me at all, and vice versa. I surely wanted to remedy that. Very soon, in fact. "Go home and change. Give me a few hours. I'm kind of tired, so I think I'll take a short nap, then clean up and I'll be ready by seven."

He still didn't look convinced, but walked me to my car. "Okay, I'll see you at seven, but if you change your mind or if you start feeling bad again, give me a call."

With that he helped me into my car and patted the hood as I drove away. I looked into the rear view mirror and once again thanked my lucky stars that I had a date with him tonight. But nothing serious, I reminded myself. Especially, no marriage. I refused to be Sam Darling O'Dear. Of course, I guessed I could keep my maiden name. When I married Alan, I did just that. His last name was Wonder, so I certainly didn't want to be Sam Darling Wonder. So I've been Sam Darling all my life. Guess I could keep that up when Michael and I got married.

This fantasy was certainly far out. Michael and I hadn't even experienced our first date and already I had decided to keep my maiden name. I better be careful and not blurt out this insanity in his presence. That would scare him off for sure.

It took all of two minutes to arrive at my castle. As I dragged myself in the door, Clancy gave me "the look."

I stripped off my wrinkled clothes and left a trail to the bathroom. I took a two-minute shower and then left a message with my wake-up service. "Listen, Clance, I don't have time to talk. Wake me up in an hour."

She didn't. But something else did.

EIGHT

THROUGH A DAZE I felt the pain begin. It started slowly and then hit in large waves that pushed me toward consciousness. I resisted opening my eyes but someone kept slapping me. I raised an eyelid, so I could see who would receive my revenge. Georgianne Granville! The old witch. I tried to slap her back, but couldn't move. Why in the world was she hitting me? Why was I lying in the snow?

"She's awake."

I opened another eye. Gus and Michael knelt by me with looks of concern on their faces. Was this how Dorothy felt in the "Wizard of Oz," when she woke up with a horrible headache and memories of a fantastic dream? But the wicked witch wasn't dead, she was here. And she was slapping me. Or at least one of the wicked witches was here. I was sure there were more. Part of my dream included a beautiful witch who was after my intended boyfriend.

"What happened?"

Gus smiled down at me, "Don't worry, honey, everything is going to be fine. You're just lucky no one lit a match. The carriage house'll be fine as soon as we air it out."

Air it out? What was he talking about? I knew that I probably had "nap breath," but I'd showered before I went to sleep and planned on brushing my teeth before my date. I suddenly remembered that I was nude the last time I looked. Unfortunately my head refused to move and I couldn't check the status of my clothing.

Michael looked at Gus, "Let's move her into your house, okay? We need to get her off the ground."

"What happened?"

"I suppose you can take her into my home, but I hope it won't be for long. Mr. Granville needs his rest you know, too much excitement can lead to…"

"Georgianne, quit jabbering and open the damn door."

Jeez, I would have paid money for this.

"What happened?" I was feeling a bit redundant by this time. It appeared that I was the star of this melodrama, but no one was paying attention to me.

"What happened?" I yelled, or more correctly, I tried to yell, but my throat hurt and my voice sounded like it used to after a night of beer and cigarettes. I felt like crap, too.

"We'll tell you everything in a minute, Sam. Right now, we're going to take you into the Granville's house. I guess we should take her dog, too." Michael glanced at Gus for permission. He probably already knew that Georgianne wouldn't roll out the welcome mat for Clancy.

"Clancy. Where is she? What happened?" That took my remaining energy and was all I remembered until I woke up on the Granville's sofa. Jill was hovering over me, playing doctor. Okay, so she is a doctor, but she's my kid sister and it's hard to take.

"What happened?" I'm nothing if not persistent. Stubborn might be a more apt description, but I was entitled to know what in the hell was going on.

Jill decided to treat me like a grown up. "There was a gas leak or something in your home and you breathed a lot of fumes. I want to take you in to the ER to check your blood gasses, run some other tests, and to keep an eye on you for a while."

Jill looked so cute and grown up with the stethoscope around her neck. Was this competent young physician my baby sister? I decided she was serious and I better obey.

"Where's Clancy?" With that I noticed that the kisses being planted on my face were not a gift from Michael as I'd fantasized, but came from my faithful companion.

Clancy seemed no worse for the wear.

"How did I get out?"

Now it was Gus's turn. "That was the darndest thing, Sam. I heard Clancy barking real loud, like she does when strangers come to your door. So I looked out the back window and didn't see anything. She was still barking, so I put on my coat and went out. At the same time this nice young man was approaching your house and we both smelled gas. Lucky I had my keys with me. I unlocked your door and we saw Clancy lying on her belly barking like crazy. This young man opened windows while I followed Clancy to you. I found you on your bed, passed out."

"My clothes?" I stammered, hoping against hope that Michael hadn't seen me nude. If I was passed out that meant I wasn't holding my stomach in.

Gus reassured me. "Don't worry, honey, I wrapped you in your grandma's quilt that was on your bed."

I glanced down, saw the quilt and felt better. Then a scream escaped my raw throat, "Eeeeyuk."

"What?" The word came from everyone at once.

"Eeeeyuk. Georgianne's housecoat. Eeeeyuk." How could they do that to me?

Georgianne seemed oblivious to my distaste. "I assumed you'd want to be modest under the quilt, so when we brought you inside I volunteered the use of my dressing gown."

I stammered my thanks, and tried to figure out how to ditch the robe as soon as possible. And to think Michael was looking at me, in clothing that clashed with every single fiber of my being.

Again I returned to the subject of my housemate, "How did Clancy survive? She weighs a few pounds less than I do."

Michael ignored my slight exaggeration. "She was splayed out on the floor by the door. Almost looked like she'd been through some military basic training and knew to stay low to the ground."

Gus continued the saga, "We brought you outside and I turned off the main gas line. Georgianne called Jill. You always tell me she's the best doctor in the city. After you came around, we carried you in here. Jill arrived a few minutes ago."

I smiled in spite of it all. So did Jill.

"I appreciate everyone's concern but I'm not going to the ER."

"Oh yes you are." Jill again.

"Oh no I'm not."

"Oh yes you are." Michael's turn.

"Oh no I'm not."

"Oh yes you…" Gus and Georgianne began in unison.

"Oh no I'm not…to infinity."

"Infinity plus one," chimed in Jill. "I win and you're going to the hospital."

"But I've got a date with Michael." This in a whining voice from the pathetic loser, me. No one heard me, or if they did, they ignored my protestations.

Finally, I decided fighting was futile. If Jill wanted me to go to "Darling Memorial" then I would.

I turned to my friend. "Gus, would you keep Clancy for me? She'd feel better close to home."

Gus said yes immediately and ignored his wife's malevolent stare. I knew he'd pay for this later, but was grateful that he dared go against Georgianne. That was true friendship. Clancy would be one less thing I'd have to worry about now.

Then I remembered Michael. "Michael, our date..." Now I was almost blubbering. Can you beat that? Not the least bit upset that I almost died, but that I was forced to miss the big date.

"That's okay. I'll cancel our reservations. I'll go with you to the hospital and I'll grab something to eat there."

I decided to be unselfish. "No, I wouldn't wish hospital food on a friend. Call me later tonight. I'm sure I'll be home before bedtime. We'll talk." I still wanted to find out some things, like what he'd been doing at Burns' office, in the ER, and at Burns' house with Carolyn.

He finally agreed with me, pecked me on the cheek

and left. Our first kiss and I felt sick. Plus smelled like gas. I just knew he'd come back for more.

Jill drove as she did everything else—confidently. "Put that blanket around you. Just relax and don't try to sit up straight. We'll be at the hospital in a few minutes." I smiled in spite of my headache. This was a nice change of roles for me, the nurturee rather than the nurturer. I could get used to this.

Jill took charge when we got there. She quickly drew blood, not waiting for a medical technologist to arrive. When she was assured of my comfort, she left.

As I was waiting in the treatment room for the results of the tests, the door opened and *he* stood there showing concern. My un-favorite detective, Butthead.

His suit looked the same—rumpled, but decent looking. I idly wondered who picked them out for him. Was he married? Who would have him? What did I ever see in him? Why was I asking myself so many questions?

Looking like a Columbo who was losing his hair, he began, "I heard you had some trouble at your house. You okay?"

"Yeah, what are you doing here?" I turned the tables on him, because I recalled that this was virtually the same question he asked me when we found Dr. Burns dead on the floor.

"Don't get all defensive on me. Gus called me because

he was concerned about the supposed gas leak at your house. Gus prides himself on running a tight ship, so he was upset, not only at you being in danger, but also because he was sure that the house was safe. I called Central Illinois Public Service, and they sent out a technician to check. There was a gas leak behind your stove, but there's a possibility that someone tampered with the line. There were a few suspicious holes in the pipe. Feeling suicidal, Sam?"

God, I wanted to wipe that grin off of his face. "You know, I'm feeling more homicidal than suicidal."

He ignored my clever jibe. "Do you know anyone that might want to see you dead? Or maybe just scare you?"

"No. There might be a few misguided souls who might not like me, but I don't think anyone would want to kill me."

He smiled that smile again. Why did he make me so mad after all these years?

He made a feeble attempt to grasp my hand, which I evaded with the skill of a commando.

"This is a serious matter." He tried to appear unaffected by my rebuff. "There's a good chance someone tried to kill you, or at the very least make you sick. I want to talk to you again tomorrow when you're feeling better. In the meantime, the gas company is working on the line and it should be fixed by morning."

Jill entered at that moment and piped in, "She can stay at my house tonight, Detective. She seems fine, but I want to keep an eye on her anyway." She went off to call her husband, Ben.

After she left, B.H. turned toward me and asked, "I'd like to ask you a personal question."

I had a horrible headache, but figured a little more agony wouldn't do any harm. "Sure."

"What's this B.H. stuff?"

I was too tired to beat around the bush. "'B.H.' stands for 'Butthead.' I thought it was more respectful to abbreviate it, so I don't embarrass you in public."

"Butthead, huh?" The smile didn't falter for long. "You sure know how to hold a grudge, don't you? You know, I didn't stand you up on purpose. Prom night was kinda important to me too. I just…"

I interrupted him; "I'm not interested in your pathetic apologies. You stood me up. You didn't call. You didn't attempt to explain. I think that says it all."

His usual cool disappeared. He looked decidedly uncomfortable. I felt great. He eyed me one last time, then turned and headed for the door. He glanced back and in a more businesslike tone said, "I'll be in touch tomorrow." With that, he was gone.

See, that's another thing I hate about men. He was the Butthead, but I felt guilty. My short-term elation at his discomfort was just that. There was a murderer still on the loose and here I was, laid up.

After arriving at Jill's, I still felt bad and decided to take a nap. A fitting ending to an overly-eventful day.

NINE

I AWOKE THE next morning to kisses. "Clancy, cut it out. I'll take you outside in a minute." Then I heard giggles that were decidedly un-Clancylike.

Jill's kids were attacking me with smooches. Jack and Marty were four and three respectively, and were bundles of energy. Jack had his mother's fair complexion and blonde hair and Marty was the spitting image of his father, Ben, with dark hair and dark eyes. Together these two kids looked like a salt and pepper set, delightful and complementary.

"Ready for breakfast, Sam?" Ben grinned at me from the kitchen doorway, brandishing a pan and spatula. A wisp of dark hair fell over his eyes. Attired in a "Kiss the Cook" apron that fit nicely over his jeans and T-shirt, he looked every inch the strong man that he was.

"Did you make your special pancakes?"

"Yep, and we got coffee and juice, too."

"Count me in." A healthy appetite was something I could always count on.

I allowed the kids to tug on me and to help pull me up from the couch and lead me to the kitchen. This was a very comfortable home. I'd been here many times, primarily because I was Jill's godmother and in our family, we took that role seriously and it was a life-long relationship.

Jill had the good fortune—and good sense—to marry a great guy. Ben was a plumber and was struggling to start his own business. He had worked for other people while Jill was in medical school, and now it was her turn to provide the major financial support while his company was in its infancy. When they were both at work, the kids stayed at Angie and Ed's. Angie provided daycare for the family. It worked out well for everyone.

Jill was already at work, so Ben said he would drop me off at my house when he took the kids to Angie's. It was Saturday, but both of them had non-traditional work schedules.

I enjoyed the breakfast and ate much more than was wise. I was wondering if I dared ask for one more flapjack when my phone interrupted me. It was Gus.

"Your house is ship-shape again and Clancy is panting for your return." It was comforting to know someone was.

Later, unlocking the door to the carriage house, it just seemed different. I normally felt so secure there. It was home. How dare someone invade my world with such potentially deadly results? Hating myself for being so weak, I felt the need to check each room, closet, and under every bed.

I began in the living room. Feeling foolish, I checked in Grandma's armoire. It was stuffed with junk, just like always. No bad guys. There was a small coat closet in the front hall. Nothing there.

On to the dining room, my office. No closets, nothing anyone could hide in. I smiled at the stack of unpaid bills on my desk. They seemed a bit inconsequential when I thought about my close call last night.

The kitchen beckoned, a room with which I had a love/hate relationship. I loved the food and hated the work. No place for a nasty person to lurk, except for the almost bare pantry. Empty. Of people, as well as food.

I turned and made my way down the short hallway to my bedroom and bath. Lots of cubbyholes and hiding places back there. I'd never been a particularly cautious person nor easily frightened, but I felt my heart rate increase. I flicked on the light switch, opened the curtains and before I could talk myself out of it I flung open the closet door and the bathroom door at the same time. I jumped out of the way immediately, just in case someone was waiting to pounce. No one pounced. I looked under the king-sized bed. No monsters there either.

A search of the two bedrooms and bathroom upstairs also revealed no bogeyman. The upstairs bath was the hardest room to search, as the music from *Psycho* and *Jaws* both played in my head at the same time.

Satisfied, I re-locked the door and slowly walked across the back lawn to Gus and Georgianne's.

Clancy greeted me in the expected way, with disdain. How dare I leave her overnight, even with someone as nice as Gus? Not to mention forcing the indignity of Georgianne on her.

I whispered, "I'll make it up to you," and thanked Georgianne for her kindness. She harrumphed, but grudgingly said I was welcome.

Gus insisted on escorting me to my house. I didn't let him know that I'd already checked it for goblins.

Clancy ran around smelling every piece of furniture and hidey-hole, just to make sure everything was okay in her fiefdom. As she bounced around, Gus whispered, "Do you think it's wise to stay here by yourself?"

"There's no need to whisper, Gus. I don't have secrets from Clancy. Besides, I'm not alone. Clancy's here and remember, she saved my life yesterday. I'll be fine, I promise. And you're just a back yard away. I swear I'll call you if I need help."

Gus finally agreed and listed several ways to contact him. He talked about bells, whistles, lights, signals, and finally agreed that the phone would be adequate until he could install an alarm which would buzz in his home if I punched a panic button that would be hooked up in several places in my house. As he turned to leave, murmuring about watts, wires, and what not, he appeared livelier than I'd seen him in years.

"I may be wrong, Gus, but you seem to be feeling a lot better. Lots of energy."

"Well, it's surprising, but with Dr. Burns dying and you almost dying, it's kind of exciting around here. I don't want to miss anything." With that he hugged me and exited.

I wanted to crash for awhile, but thought I'd check my messages. I wasn't surprised to find the message light blinking frantically.

Beep. "It's Jen. Jill told me what happened. If you need anything let me know. Love you."

Beep. "Sam, Ed. Glad you're okay. Angie sends her love. Talk to you later."

Beep. "I'm praying for you." Pete. "Call me when you can."

Beep. "I know I just saw you a few minutes ago," Jill's maternal voice made me smile, "but I wanted to make sure you were all right. Don't forget to come into the office on Monday."

Beep. "Sam. Rob. Glad you're okay. Don't worry

about Dr. Burns' killer. We'll get him soon. And if someone did sabotage your gas line, we'll find him too. Take care."

Beep. "Hey, Mom." Sarah. "Aunt Jill told us you were okay, so we're not worried. We both want to know how you get yourself in these messes. Sometimes I feel like the Mom instead of the kid. Adam sends his love too. We'll call again later. Get some rest."

Two final messages.

Beep. "Sam, this is George Lansing." B.H. "I'd like to come by your place around three if that's okay. I want to talk about a few things. See ya then."

Beep. "Hello. This is Michael O'Dear. I hope you're feeling better. I'd like to stop by later today to see you. Maybe we can have dinner. Give me a call when you get a chance."

It looked like I would be spending as much time with B.H. as with Michael. Yuck. Maybe I could make an appointment with the honorable detective and then not show up. Fitting revenge after all these years.

Clancy kept looking at me, as if I weren't keeping my end of the bargain. "I promise we'll walk later, Clancy. Georgianne said that she hired someone to take you for a long walk and you were gone over an hour. So don't try to make me feel guilty for not going. We'll go out later. I need to rest." She halfheartedly accepted this compromise, but I had a feeling I'd pay for it later.

Before climbing into bed, I left a message for B.H. saying that 3:00 would be convenient. Same message for Michael, although with more warmth in my voice, and a different time. I told him to come by around 7, and we could go to dinner. Then, last but not least, I sent an email through my on-line service for most of my sibs and my kids—the most common way we stayed in touch. Confident that I had tied up the loose ends of my life, I turned up the heat, removed all my clothing, and climbed into bed. One of the nurturing things in my life was Grandma's quilt, guaranteed to make the scary things disappear.

When I woke up two hours later, I was famished. There were still a few more hours until B.H. would arrive to interview—or interrogate—me, so I decided to go to the market for some groceries. I put on my gray sweatpants and navy St. Francis U. sweatshirt, pulled on my boots and parka and was ready to roll. The nap had soothed my soul; now I needed something to soothe my stomach.

Clancy climbed in the car too, temporarily satisfied. This did not count as a walk, but at least it was an outing. Backing out into the alley—a horrible term for this upscale neighborhood—was always a precarious chore at best. It was difficult to see in either direction because of the many trees and bushes and because of the carriage house itself, built flush with the alley. When the trees were winter-bare I could see a little better, but not much. So I did my usual back-up, glancing in both directions and then flooring it. It had snowed and then warmed up a bit, so the asphalt road was slick, and I slid around a little.

Clancy yelped.

"Hey, leave me alone. You're the one who wanted to come along."

I'm a confident driver. That doesn't mean I'm competent, just confident. I drive with alacrity, with aplomb, with speed. Normally I drive quickly through the alley, because other than the occasional garbage truck, traffic is sparse. There was no problem as I accelerated toward Sixteenth Street. The problem was stopping.

I saw the garbage truck a split second before I heard it. I stepped on the brake and felt the pedal depress all the way to the floor. I don't remember which I said first—"Darn it," or "Sorry, Clancy." Then blackness.

This was getting pretty old and so was I. My body felt like it had been run over by a truck. Not far from the truth. I opened my eyes and saw Jill's face looking down at me.

"We gotta stop meeting like this, Dr. Jill."

"Sam, just relax. You're okay. Your car hit a garbage

truck in the alley. The truck driver is fine too. Any more questions?"

"Yeah, but I can't talk now…" I slept.

When I woke up she was still there.

I continued the conversation, "Yeah, I do have one question. Who messed up my car? I bet if you look you'll see the brakes lines are cut or something."

A grunting sound came from the corner. I tried to move my head but it hurt too much. Sooner than I would have liked, B.H. sauntered into view.

"You okay?" He actually looked like he cared. Good actor.

"Yeah, I'm fine, if you don't count the sledgehammers going full bore into my brain. Where's Clancy? She okay? Did you check the brakes on my car?"

"Clancy's fine. Gus has her." He looked a bit sheepish. "And actually we didn't check your brakes. We didn't suspect foul play, so we arranged for your car to go to the body shop. Well, anyway, I thought I'd help and I had the body shop pick up your car." He had the good grace to stop talking when I gave him the look.

"Darn it, B.H., someone sabotaged my car. The brakes didn't work. It wasn't just the ice and I wasn't speeding. Well, not much anyway. You can just tell the difference. Somebody screwed with my car and now we won't be able to tell."

"I'll call the shop right away, Sam. And remind me not to do anything nice for you." With a meager grunt, he left. I'd have to tell Georgianne to give B.H. "harrumphing" lessons. He wasn't nearly as talented as she was in that regard.

I looked at Jill. "If he didn't suspect foul play, then what was he doing here?"

"He heard the ambulance call over the radio and came in to see how you were. He was here as a friend, Sam, not as a cop."

That motherly tone crept into her voice again. If I was the older sister, why did she always use that tone with me?

The doctor persona replaced the motherly/sisterly one. "I want to keep you overnight. I don't think there'll be any complications, but this wreck, coupled with the gas incident yesterday, has really assaulted your body. You need a night of uninterrupted sleep."

Of course, I didn't like the idea. I wanted my date with Michael and I was going to have my date with Michael.

"I'm sorry but I just can't stay. I've got too much to do."

"You're staying and there'll be no discussion, argument, or whining. You were unconscious twice in less than twenty-four hours. That's hard on anyone, but at your age…" She was smart enough to stop before she finished the sentence.

"Okay, okay." I knew when I was licked.

"Oh, by the way, that Michael guy called and said he'd drop by later to see you."

Satisfied that she'd cowed me into submission, Jill left to tie up some loose ends on her shift. That gave me time to think about what was going on. What *was* going on? First, I got the job I wanted. Then immediately after hiring me, my boss was killed. Two people basically confessed, Gwen and her brother, and I was convinced neither one of them was guilty, although Gwen was sitting in jail. Then the next day, I went to Dr. Burns' house and met his wife, Carolyn. My bodily reactions convinced me she was the killer. I fainted, went home, inhaled gas, went to the ER, spent the night at Jill's, came home, got in a wreck, and ended up at the hospital again. Gee, what's wrong with this picture?

Someone had killed Burns and now, for all intents and purposes, someone had almost killed me. Were these things related? Or was this a completely different murder scheme? All of this was severely trying my patience, not to mention my mental capacity. So I did what any sane woman would do. I forgot about "whodunit" while I tidied up for Michael's visit.

TEN

MY FACE WAS bruised, my mouth felt like Clancy's smelled, and I was tired, tired, tired. I grimaced at the mirror in the sterile hospital bathroom. Combing my hair was a real chore. Each brush stroke caused my teeth to grit, causing my head to hurt, causing my teeth to grit, causing my head to...I was getting dizzy from even thinking about the cause and effect of the situation. Luckily, I kept my hair short—I kept it blonde, too—so I didn't have to spend much time on it. I decided against makeup, as I didn't want to look as sluttish as Mrs. Burns. Today, slamming her didn't feel as good, but I couldn't stop.

I had just finished gently brushing my teeth and maneuvering my way back into bed when Michael peeked around the door. The sight of him brought with it lightheadedness. Ah, romance. He had a grin on his face, a bouquet in one hand, and champagne in the other. As his grin broadened, he motioned to someone in the hallway to follow him into the room.

As I sat dumbfounded, a waiter walked in pushing a table laden with food. I'd forgotten how hungry I was, but soon remembered as he lifted the lids off trays of pasta primavera, antipasto, garlic bread, and salad. One of my favorite meals and it was catered by one of my favorite restaurants, the Rectory.

"I figured the hospital would be trying to force feed you a bland diet, so…" Michael grinned, as proud of this maneuver as if he had executed a perfect "10" on the parallel bars. And he deserved to be proud. A fantastic coup—he captured my heart and my stomach with the same feat.

I watched as the waiter, with a goofy grin on his face, took the covers off the platters and set up the table.

This was virtually a dream come true for me. A man, handsome and intelligent, actually liked me. A man, romantic and kind, sat on my bed and was about to kiss me. Women have killed for this scenario. I moistened my lips, closed my eyes, prepared for the pucker, and wouldn't you know it—the dizziness intensified.

"Michael, help."

He leaned toward me. Just in time. The good part was that I didn't have far to fall.

This scenario could have come straight out of a romance novel. I actually swooned. Michael did give me a nice place to land though.

"Are you all right? Should I call the nurse?" He helped me lie back on the pillows.

I tried pathetically to sound romantic, "No, I'm fine, just a little lightheaded. Probably from the accident." I smoothed my hair and puckered my lips again.

Michael didn't succumb to my womanly wiles. "Guess I better go if you aren't feeling well. Should I leave the food?"

I didn't know which I wanted more—Michael or the pasta. After a brief internal struggle I knew I wanted both. "Michael, don't go. We can still enjoy the food. I can't believe you did all this for me. I'd really like you to stay."

He reddened a little and said, "I hate to admit this, but I don't like hospitals. Don't take this personally, but I think we ought to postpone our meal together until you're better."

Drat. There I was, reclining in bed and I still couldn't get a kiss out of the guy. Of course, I was bruised and had on the hospital-gown-from-hell, but I wanted him to stay.

Michael spoke to the waiter, "How about leaving the food for an hour or so?" He handed the young man a folded bill.

"Sure thing, Mr. O'Dear." As he turned to leave, I swear the waiter winked at me.

I batted my eyes at Michael, but it didn't work. He took both my hands in his and said, "I'm sorry you don't feel well. But it was good to see you just the same."

Michael leaned over; I closed my eyes and prepared for the inevitable. Instead of giving me the passionate kiss I'd fantasized about, he planted a light one on my forehead. Right on a bruise.

The dizziness returned, but I didn't tell Michael.

Before he left, Michael pulled the table over to my bed, and he helped me sit up with my feet dangling over the side. His smile as he exited gave me almost as big a thrill as the feast before me.

As I ate I pondered my latest calamity. Why in the world was my equilibrium in such a state of upheaval around Michael? I really liked this guy, although I hardly knew him. And I desperately wanted to know him.

It seemed strange that every time I was near him I got dizzy. Maybe I was just scared of a relationship. Maybe I had Meniere's disease. Maybe I was allergic to Michael. Maybe I was obsessing again. So I pushed the tray aside and slept.

It had been years since I'd been in a hospital for an overnight stay. It was almost comforting that so much of the routine was the same. A smiling, nurturing nurse woke me up to give me a sleeping pill. Something clanging in the next room woke me again. Although the plastic bedpans were quieter than the old metal ones, I pictured some sadistic person in white making them clang anyway. Then a much too perky nurse roused me as she checked my blood pressure. I needed to get home so I could rest.

When I woke up the next morning, the restaurant table was gone. The waiter must have been much quieter than the nurses.

It was Sunday. I told the charge nurse I wanted to go to Mass. An aide helped me dress and insisted on delivering me to the chapel in a wheelchair. I insisted that I walk. I won.

Over the years, there'd been many changes in my life, but attending Mass wasn't one of them. Our parents had instilled that faith in us, and I felt connected when I was in church. Connected not only to people all over the world, but also to my ancestors.

As I walked into the chapel, I noticed Pete was already there, arranging things on the altar. He was on the night shift this weekend and was just coming off duty. Pete was still a priest in good standing, but was on a temporary leave from his priestly assignment. He was allowed and even encouraged to use his "priestly faculties" and often helped out at the hospital with Mass and bringing Communion to bedridden patients. I dearly loved going to Mass when he was the celebrant. What a blessing to have a brother who was a priest, and a friend, too.

"Father Brother." I smiled when I thought about how he got that name. When Pete was ordained, Rob was a teenager and didn't like the idea that everybody was calling his brother "Father." I tried to explain, but Rob started crying. When we asked him what was wrong, he said, "I don't want him to be my father, I want him to still be my brother." At that, Pete put his hand on his little brother's shoulder and told him, "I'll be your brother and I'll be Father, too. You can still call me Pete, okay?" And Rob said, "Hey, you can be my Father Brother." That's how he got the name. And it stuck.

Pete hugged me gently during the sign of peace and flashed a grin when he gave me Communion. The Chapel only held a handful of people, so the service was short.

During the closing hymn—which Pete led in a booming, slightly off-key baritone—he looked toward me and raised an eyebrow. That was the sign he wanted to talk.

After another gentle hug Pete said, "You're looking pretty energetic for someone who's been gassed and hit by a truck."

I thanked him, took his arm, and asked if he'd walk me back to my room. The bravado I'd shown by coming here without a wheelchair had been replaced by a painful exhaustion. I ached everywhere.

Pete adjusted his pace to mine. "What's up with the murder investigation?"

"Nothing much. I know Carolyn Burns killed her husband," I looked at Pete to see if he would make fun of me, "but I think she had an accomplice."

Pete didn't say anything, but he placed his hand on top of my own.

I continued, "There's something about her books that bugs me. They're good; maybe they're too good. I mean, she's not in the mental health field, but she writes as if she is. And Dr. Burns didn't seem like the kind of guy who would have helped her with those details. I looked and the acknowledgements in her books didn't thank anyone for helping."

Pete pressed the button to summon the elevator. "What does Rob say?"

"I think he's been avoiding me. You know he doesn't want me involved in the investigation."

"You can see his point, I'm sure." He held the elevator door open for me. "You really don't have any reason to be snooping."

"Now you're turning on me too?"

"Nope," he gave my hand a squeeze. "I just don't want you getting hurt. And I don't want you to get in Rob and George's way. I was wrong to encourage you earlier, Sam.

It appears someone broke into your house and tried to kill you. I don't know what I would have done if they'd been successful."

My anger dissolved into mush. I couldn't stay mad at Pete. We left the elevator and strolled to my room in a companionable silence.

After Pete left I waited for Jill to discharge me. I felt sore and knew that was just temporary. But I was still pissed off that someone had tried to kill me. Why in the world would someone want to see me dead? Tampering with the gas line in the house and the brake lines in the car had an almost deadly symmetry to it.

Since I hadn't planned on a hospital stay, I hadn't packed any of my books. To kill time, I settled in a chair, turned on the TV, and numbed my mind with the Beverly Hillbillies.

My enjoyment ended abruptly when my own private Jethro walked in.

"How ya doin', Sam?"

I kept my attention on the television. I mumbled, "What do you want, B.H.?" What was wrong with me? Why was I so mean to him? My tendency to hold grudges was my least favorite attribute.

"Wanted to see how you were doing, and also let you know that we got Dr. Burns' autopsy results. Just what we thought. He died from the blood loss from something sharp that someone stuck in his neck. Something like a knife or a scalpel. Hit his jugular vein and it was just like Niagara Falls. Swoosh." He accompanied his narrative with suitable charades, hands scraping across his neck and face grimacing as he mimicked the death throes.

He finally got my attention and I smiled without wanting to. "You sound absolutely gleeful."

"Sorry." He behaved long enough to look uncomfortable. "Interesting thing. The killer knew how to use the instrument. It was a precise cut. Rather than sideways, the cut went up and down the vein. Very effective. Very lethal. Messy too."

I didn't say anything, but the wheels were turning. B.H. said the cut was messy. I wondered how the murderer got out of Burns' office without leaving a bloody trail. I remembered that the footprints in the snow leading away from the window were clean. No blood outside. Had the cops thought about that?

I'd find out. "You said the cut was messy. Do you think the murderer was covered in blood?"

"None of your business." He dismissed my question quickly. "Anyway I want to talk to you about your mishaps."

"Yes," I tried to sound open, but failed. My basic distrust of B.H. kept leaking through. I'd figure out the blood angle on my own.

"Tell me why you think your car was sabotaged." He jerked me back to the present with his question.

"What do you mean, 'think'? It felt like the brake lines were cut or something. They went out. Slammed all the way to the floor. I know someone messed with them."

He tried to sit on the edge of my bed, but I moved my leg there so he slipped off. He recovered quickly and continued the conversation. "When you said the brakes went out you were right. They were in bad shape, but show no signs of tampering. I spoke to the mechanic myself."

"But..."

B.H. held out a hand in a "stop" fashion. "And before you tell me that the mechanic was in on the plot to get you, I want to tell you that the mechanic is your cousin, Bobby."

"Well..."

"Do you have any other reason to think your car was tampered with? Did anyone threaten you?" B.H. sat in the only chair available.

"Well, no, but since I'm on the trail of the murderer, I'm sure someone is after me, and..." I didn't want to let him in on my certainty that Carolyn Burns committed the crime.

"Rob and I told you to stay out of it and let us handle the case. You're a social worker, not a cop."

This was beginning to get boring. Everyone kept telling me what my job was.

"Well, listen here, what about the gas in my house? You said that was deliberate."

The stop sign went up again. "The man from the gas company said the line *might* have been cut. 'Might have been cut' is a long way from 'was cut.'"

"Don't you dare give me the 'talk to the hand' sign." I threw a pillow at him and instantly regretted it for two reasons. First, it hurt like hell and second, it only made him chuckle. "You think you know everything. Just get out of here."

"Uh-uh. Not until you tell me what you know about the murder."

I relented a bit. "I'll tell you what I know if you tell me what you know."

He grinned. "Didn't we say that to each other in fifth grade when we found out how babies were made? I went into the 'guy' movie with Fr. MacGregor and you went to the 'girl' movie with Sr. Mary Francis."

I scowled. "Yeah, I remember. And it wasn't long after that you said, 'You show me yours and I'll show you mine.'"

"You never did show me."

I was triumphant. "And I never will."

"Seriously, Sam. I need to find out what you know

and what you think you know. And I promise I'll tell you what I can. Deal?"

"Yeah, uh, okay." I sighed. Loudly.

"Oh, I guess you don't feel too good, huh? Maybe we can talk later. How about tomorrow? Maybe we can have dinner or something."

"Yeah, right. And I'll wear my prom dress."

"Sam..."

I sighed again and added a groan for good measure. "Okay, that was a little much, I admit."

He took that as a dismissal and left.

My last conscious thought before I dozed off again was that I'd have to figure out how the murderer escaped being bloody. My dreams were a kaleidoscope of prom dresses and bloody scalpels.

ELEVEN

JILL DISCHARGED ME late Sunday afternoon with admonitions to be careful. I refused her offer of a wheelchair to the parking lot, but lost that battle. She passed me to a smiling aide with a shiny wheelchair. And before I could murmur much more than "good-bye and thanks," I was whisked away faster than you could say "Indianapolis 500." We quickly reached the parking lot and when the aide asked which car was mine, I didn't know. B.H. had gotten a rental car for me while mine was being repaired. Nice gesture, and it almost started melting this cold, cold heart. I looked on the key chain and noted the rental was a generic little sedan. New. Automatic. No character. This car was nothing like my baby. I had a '68 Volkswagen Beetle. A classic. With character. After a row by row search, we found a license plate that matched the one on the key chain. Even though I was unimpressed with the vehicle, today my poor muscles could appreciate the power steering and automatic transmission.

I drove home, picked up Clancy from Gus's house, and spent the rest of the day alternating between resting and apologizing to Clancy. She must be a Catholic dog; she's got the guilt trip down pat. I did manage to take her for a short, and slow, walk. After that tiring exercise, I slept. And slept.

I woke up at 8 AM on Monday to a dog with a leash in her mouth. "Okay, girl, I've got time for a short walk and that's all. I've got a funeral to go to."

Clancy didn't argue the point. She waited patiently while I donned my sweat pants and jacket.

We walked a few blocks west on Maine Street. I was grateful the ice had melted on the sidewalks. There was still some snow on the lawns, forming a perfect frame for the Victorian mansions on our street.

"Thanks for walking slowly today, girl. I'm still stiff from the accident. But you don't seem to feel any bad effects." I swear she started limping. "Nice try, but you won't get any sympathy from me."

After turning around and re-tracing our steps, we reached our little corner of heaven about 20 minutes after we began.

"I promise a longer walk tomorrow. And I'll try to go a little faster too." We both smiled. "I've got to get ready for the funeral. I wouldn't miss this show for the world."

As I unhooked Clancy's leash, I continued, "Even

though B.H. said no one is out to get me, I'm not convinced that the gas line and my car wreck were accidents. I have a feeling about this and I'm going to trust my instincts."

Clancy jumped on the bed and watched while I gingerly climbed into my closet again, looking for the perfect outfit. Classy, yet understated. Demure, yet attractive. I knew Michael would be at the funeral, and if I could hold my vertigo long enough, I'd find out what his connection was to Dr. and Mrs. Burns.

I found I couldn't concentrate on clothes yet and turned to my confidante. "I can't believe that Felicia Greene is Carolyn Burns. Doesn't that just jerk your chain? My favorite novelist is my least favorite villain. How can I love those books so much and hate the author? Doesn't seem logical."

I continued the conversation thread, although silently. Carolyn's books were psychological thrillers, dealing with psychotic and mentally ill murderers. I smiled as I contemplated Carolyn Burns as the model for all the villains in her books. I thought about re-reading her books, trying to get inside her criminal mind. I left the bedroom and semi-limped through the house, gathering up Felicia Greene's books as I went. They formed two good-sized stacks next to my bed; but looking through them would have to wait. I needed to get back to the important business at hand—what to wear.

The only decent thing I had was my power suit. I certainly didn't want to wear it again. Just because it was the only good thing I owned didn't mean I wanted people to know it. I got creative. I took an old black cocktail dress and added a black blazer. Looked pretty good. And fit my criteria: classy, understated, demure. Michael would be an idiot not to be attracted to me.

I drove to the church for the funeral Mass. The majority of people in Quincy are Catholic. Even bad guys. As I arrived I was surprised to note that the parking lot was nearly full, although it was early. Like most in my family, I'm compulsively early. Always want to get a good seat.

The church was pretty full, for a Monday, and for a funeral Mass. I found a seat toward the front. I wanted to see the action. None of my family was there, so it was easy to find a solitary seat.

I knelt to pray and felt someone looking at me. Across the aisle I saw a grinning Gus. I nodded and discreetly waved. Georgianne was sitting regally beside her husband. I nodded to her also, while keeping a nonchalant expression. It was hard not to laugh, though. She pictured herself as one of the ruling class and pompously looked down her nose as much as the Burns' butler.

Right before Mass started, Carolyn Burns was escorted up the aisle by none other than Michael O'Dear. Luckily, I'd prepared myself for the shock, so only felt a distant dizziness and wasn't in danger of getting sick. I think I'd be too scared to do that anyway, remembering the ridicule afforded to those kids who fainted or hurled in church during my school years.

"Hi ya, Sam."

He was making a habit of interrupting my pleasant thoughts. It was no surprise that he couldn't even leave me alone when I was praying, or almost praying.

"Hey, B.H." I'm nice in church.

He leaned over and whispered, "So, you goin' out to the cemetery?"

"Yeah."

"So you goin' to Burns' house?" He tried to enter the pew.

"Yeah." I didn't let him.

"Can I go with you?" He tried again.

"No." I didn't budge, ignoring the stares of those around us.

He stopped whispering. "Sam, let me go. I need to go, but can't go as a cop. Everyone would clam up. I gotta go with a friend. C'mon."

"Okay, but two things. Number one, you must tell me some of the stuff you know."

"And two?"

My voice finally rose above a whisper. "Number two is you can't, under penalty of death, pretend you're my date. Got it? That is vitally important."

He grinned. "Afraid O'Dear will get jealous."

I didn't let him make me mad. "Yes or no?"

"Yes, but it looks like O'Dear is pretty busy with Mrs. Burns."

"Getting smart with me will not get you invited." I returned the intimidating look of a dowager in front of me.

"Okay, Sam. We're just old friends and that's the way I'll play it."

"Okay." I tired of being mean, finally relented, and allowed him to join me in the pew.

I resumed my reverent posture. It wasn't entirely for B.H.'s benefit. I was praying that Michael would like me best.

B.H. and I called a temporary truce and stood, knelt, and sat on cue. I found it hard to concentrate during Mass and wondered if Carolyn would like to trade "dates" with me. B.H. could be her bodyguard—they deserved each other—and Michael could sit with me. Of course, I didn't act on my impulse. The ghost of Sister Nicholas was a strong presence in that church and I could just picture her with hands on her hips, threatening me with eternal purgatory if I didn't pay attention during Mass.

When the service ended, Michael and Carolyn walked down the aisle following the casket. Michael saw me and mouthed something. It looked like, "I love you, Sam," but I couldn't swear to that. Maybe I was fantasizing again. Maybe what he really mouthed was, "I want to talk to you."

The town's Catholic cemetery was only a few miles away. In small towns, distance is measured by miles and not by minutes. You know that if the distance is ten miles and you drive 60 mph it will take you ten minutes. If you drive 30 mph it will take you twenty minutes. It's simple in a location that has no real rush hour. In fact, rush hour in Quincy meant we all drove fast to miss the train at the crossing and also miss all the tractors on the highway.

We got in my car.

"Listen, B.H., I never really thanked you for taking my car to the shop and getting this car for me."

"You still haven't."

"Okay, thanks." That was hard.

"See that wasn't so bad was it? You're welcome."

"Put your seatbelt on or we won't go anywhere." I used my best "mommy voice" for this.

He complied and sarcastically thanked me for caring about his well being.

I pulled into line behind a Mercedes. "We've only got a few minutes. I really want to talk to you."

"Hey, that's my line. I need to talk to you too. I want to find out what you know..." He relaxed into the generic seat of the generic rental.

"And tell me what you know."

"And tell you *some* of what I know."

I relented. "Okay, here's the deal. You and I can go to dinner tomorrow night. You buy. Separate cars. Don't tell anyone. No touching."

"Deal. Let's go to The Rectory."

The Rectory had nothing to do with the church. It was a popular restaurant and watering hole located close to St. Francis University. Stained glass windows were the closest it got to church related matters. Most of the students from SFU hung out there. The downside was that it was in my old neighborhood and I was sure to see people I knew. The upside was that it had the best onion rings in town and cheap beer.

"I'll meet you there. Six o'clock, tomorrow night. Now that's Tuesday, George."

"I know, Sam. And thanks for calling me George."

Like he cares. He hadn't objected to my calling him B.H. And he kept acting like a Butthead.

At that moment we pulled up behind the line of cars at the cemetery and Michael came over to the window. I didn't have the opportunity to tell B.H. that I'd called him "George" accidentally. But if it made him feel better, I would continue. Maybe I could get more information from him that way.

I spent a few minutes smiling at Michael as I struggled to get the window down. It wouldn't budge. I felt stupid and was sure that Michael did not find my struggle attractive.

"You have to have the engine running to use the automatic windows."

"Shut up, George."

I stopped bothering with the window and opened the door. Michael seemed glad to see me and the feeling was very mutual. I explained to him that George just needed a ride and then patiently waited for him to explain why he was with Carolyn Burns. He didn't.

"Michael, why are you with Mrs. Burns?"

"Carolyn asked me to accompany her. She has no family and since the murderer is still at large, she feels a little uncertain and alone. So she hired me to be her bodyguard as well as investigate the murder. Any more questions?"

God, he was gorgeous.

"No, just curious. But I told you she's the murderer. And I need you to believe me. She killed her husband."

George leaned over the console and said, "Sam thinks

she knows everything about the murder. In fact she…"

I slammed the door in his face without acknowledging his childish taunt.

Michael seemed interested. "How do you know that?"

"I just know and I can't tell you why. At least not here. I'll tell you later. Tonight. Do you think we can have dinner, after the thing at Burns' house?"

"That sounds like a good idea. I'll see if one of my men can take over. Right now I need to be with Carolyn. See you at her house later?"

I smiled and nodded. I also tried to control the dizzy feeling that the thought of Carolyn Burns brought on.

After Michael left, George got out of the car with another stupid grin in evidence. He had quite a repertoire of ignorant looks.

I wanted to be silent, but couldn't. "What?"

"What do you mean, 'what?'"

"What are you grinning at?"

"Nothing," he lied. "Just smiling."

George and I walked over well-tended graves and settled at the edge of the large crowd. He watched everyone and I watched Michael. And Carolyn. I mean, I'm a nice person and normally I'd feel sympathy for a woman whose husband has just been killed. But, my God, she killed him and I couldn't feel any sorrow for her. Not only did she kill her husband, but she was also trying to steal my boyfriend. My potential boyfriend anyway.

The burial was strictly by the book. Almost everyone from the church was at the cemetery. I didn't know if they were there out of respect for Dr. Burns or because murders were rare in Quincy.

The priest said lots of familiar phrases. "Pillar of the community." "Quincy's loss." "Sympathy to Mrs. Burns." "Meet in heaven." And so on. Heard it before. Too many times.

It was cold. The wind whipped around the tent and people huddled together, whether from grief or from the cold, I couldn't tell. I snuggled down into my coat and thought about how Burns died. Sliced in the neck with a scalpel. It was an ignominious end for a doctor.

The memory of Burns' phone conversation while I was waiting in the hall for my interview suddenly surfaced and caused me to hit myself in the forehead. I grimaced as I made contact with a still-tender spot. "Damn!" Heads turned to stare at my outburst. "Sorry," I whispered to no one in particular.

I swear George chuckled. It was almost enough for me to call him B.H. again.

My interview with Dr. Burns had interrupted a phone call. Who had he been talking to? He said, "I'll have it for you next week." After a few moments he'd blurted,

"Leave me alone or you'll be sorry." That didn't sound like something he would say to his wife.

I was sure she killed him. Absolutely one hundred percent sure. But that didn't mean she had done it alone. She could have had an accomplice. Maybe that's who Burns had been talking to that morning. I'd mentioned this to George right after the murder, then promptly forgot about it. I wondered if he remembered. I'd bring it up again tomorrow night, after he gave me some tidbits.

After the burial, George and I joined the many cars heading out to Burns' house. The sedan seemed out of place amidst the Mercedes, BMWs, Range Rovers, and Porsches. Earlier I'd thought that the nondescript car would be ideal for a stakeout. But not in this crowd. It stood out like a Darling at a Debutante Ball.

We got to the house and went inside. I didn't even hesitate as the butler took our coats and led us into the drawing room. I was getting used to this.

George tried to take my arm. "No way. Remember our deal. I said you could come with me and we'd walk in together. We're here now and you're on your own. And I specifically said 'no touching.'"

"Sorry, Sam. Guess I forgot your rules." Was he being sarcastic or sincere? I couldn't tell and I didn't care.

I separated from George at the first opportunity and looked around for Michael. He and Carolyn Burns were conspicuous by their absence. I wanted to talk to him, and look at him, so I started nosing around. I had a cover story all prepared. If questioned, I'd say that I was looking for a bathroom. That wasn't original, and perhaps I didn't think it through very thoroughly, but I thought it would work. After all, we were at a wake and people certainly wouldn't suspect me of any nefarious activity. So I ventured into the kitchen. No one there. I grabbed a few snacks off a silver tray and went up the back stairs.

At the top of the stairs lay two small bedrooms. Probably servants' rooms originally. One was made into a sewing room and the other contained a treadmill, stair stepper and weights. The far wall was covered with a floor-to-ceiling mirror. I bet Carolyn Burns spent hours staring at herself.

Next was a bathroom. After that, two doors on either side of the hall led to two larger bedrooms, both a little too frou-frou for my taste. At the far end, past the front staircase, was a closed door. Probably the master suite. It looked like it took up the whole front of the house.

As I stood there wondering if I should go inside, I heard voices. Those voices needed listening to, so I volunteered.

No one was around so I pressed my ear against the door.

"Listen, if you just keep your mouth shut, nothing will happen. There is no proof and there won't be any proof. Just shut up and we won't have any problems." That sounded like Carolyn. Sure didn't sound so refined and uppity now.

"Mumble, mumble."

I'd heard that mumbling voice before. Who was it?

"I beg your pardon, Ma'am. May I help you?"

The butler.

"Yes, I was looking for the bathroom."

"It's down the hall, Madam. Would you like me to show you?"

"Certainly not." I tried to "harrumph" but couldn't quite pull it off. So I sashayed to the bathroom.

TWELVE

I AVOIDED GEORGE but noticed he managed to speak to a lot of people and apparently didn't ruffle any feathers. Being from Quincy had its advantages. He was "one of us" and could get away with being a guest—and a pest—without attracting undue attention.

Once I found Gus, he made my visit palatable. We sat on a couch and he entertained me with stories about our fellow guests. He speculated on possible suspects and motives. I wasn't ready to let him in on my absolute assurance that Carolyn did it, but I did want to know what he thought.

"Who do you think killed Dr. Burns?" I tried to make the question sound innocent.

"Well, I've been thinking about it and he wasn't a very popular character. He's been involved in some shady business deals and..."

I interrupted, "Shady business deals? What kind?"

Gus continued as if I hadn't spoken, "...he's treated lots of folks pretty badly. I've heard complaints about his therapy practice too, but for years he was the only game in town." He moved on to another thought. "You told me you don't think Gwen Schneider did it. Have you changed your opinion? Everyone's talking about how she confessed to you."

"I'm sure she didn't do it. For lots of reasons, including that she didn't have a motive. She and the doctor were close. Very close." I raised my eyebrows and elbowed Gus in the ribs so he would understand my meaning. "Also her brother Charlie confessed and I'm equally sure he didn't do it."

Gus grinned at my hint, but then became serious when he asked, "Why are you so sure that Charlie Schneider didn't do it?"

"I'm just sure. Let's talk about something else; what did you mean Burns was involved in shady business deals?"

Gus bit into a mini-quiche, chewed for a moment, swallowed, and took a sip from his beer before answering. "Nothing in particular, just heard some things that told me he wasn't on the up-and-up. Insider trading, prescriptions for friends without examining them, things like that."

That wasn't worth waiting for. Then the conversation took a turn for the worse when he changed the subject to Carolyn Burns.

"You've read her books, right?"

"You know I don't read trash." I said it with a straight face, but Gus is not easily fooled by my fabrications.

"You already told me you've read her books. And just because you don't like her, doesn't mean her books aren't worthwhile." He smiled at me as one does at a much-loved, but errant child.

"Okay," I grudgingly admitted, "I've read a few…"

Gus stared at me, unbelieving and silent.

"All right, I've read all of them. I didn't like them much."

The maddening silence and stare continued.

"God, Gus, stop with the third degree, will you? I read them all and I liked them all, but that was before I knew Felicia Greene is Carolyn Burns." Blecch! I still shivered at the thought that Carolyn Burns wrote the books that had been scattered all over my house.

An idea struck and I almost pounded on my fellow crime solver. "You know, one reason I like the books so much is that they're realistic. I mean the criminal mind with its emotional disturbances…it's almost as if the author was either a therapist, a criminal, or crazy herself." Two out of three wasn't bad.

"You think she killed her husband?"

Hesitantly I nodded, not sure of exactly what to say.

"You think she's crazy, Sam?" Gus's raised eyebrows

and squinted eyes showed he obviously didn't.

"Maybe not crazy, but she's evil. She had to have an accomplice and that accomplice must be a therapist or psychiatrist."

Gus didn't bother to swallow his current canapé as he blurted, "An accomplice in writing the books? Or in murder?"

I thought for a second before answering. "Maybe both. Someone had to help her with the details in the books. And she doesn't have a medical background, so how did she know to slice the vein lengthwise?"

Gus replied, "Hearing all that, it would seem more logical that she didn't have anything to do with the murder."

"You surprise me, Gus."

He put his arm around my shoulder. "Now, I'm not saying you're wrong. I'm just suggesting you keep your mind open to other possibilities."

"Yeah, yeah. But she did it. Really she did. She is just evil."

"Do your feelings about Carolyn Burns have anything to do with your young fellow?"

I immediately and adroitly changed the subject again. Gus followed suit; after all he was my friend. He took my mind off Michael and Carolyn for a while. I sat and basked in his wit and warmth.

Finally my patience was rewarded and Michael approached me.

"Hi, Sam. Gus."

Gus echoed my hello.

Michael's look made me smile. "Can we talk for a minute?" I nodded. "We can go in the kitchen."

Of course, I'm sure Carolyn never goes in there. "Sure, Michael. Gus, I'll see you at home." I winked at Gus as I walked away.

Michael led me into the kitchen. So far, so good. I was only feeling a slight dizziness. And except for ingesting a couple slugs of pink stomach-soother, I hadn't eaten anything except the snacks I grabbed on my reconnaissance mission.

Michael turned as he spoke. "I know you have a lot of questions. And I do too. Can you hold them until dinner tonight?"

"Yeah, I guess. But this time, we're going to dinner even if I'm in a cast from head to toe."

"I agree. It certainly appears that the fates are conspiring against us. How about if we go for an early meal? I'll follow you home from here and pick you up right away. That way there'll be no chance of anything new happening to you."

"Sounds good to me. By the way, where've you been the last hour or so? I looked for you."

"Oh, you did?" He grinned as if he found that thought appealing. "I was around. We've just installed a new security system and I was checking it out, plus I was meeting with one of my associates about taking over for me tonight."

"Oh, I thought you might have been with Carolyn."

"No, in fact I haven't seen much of her since we got back from the cemetery." He stepped aside as a bejeweled and bewigged matron passed by. "Why did you think I'd be with her?"

"Dunno. Just thought, since you're her bodyguard that you'd be with her." I moved as the woman realized she was in the kitchen of all places and beat a hasty exit.

"Well, we decided she'd be safe here. I think she wasn't feeling well and went up to her room."

"Is that the big room at the front of the house?" I gestured in the general direction.

"Yeah, it's the master suite, why?"

"Just curious." I promptly changed the subject, because I didn't want to discuss my nefarious activities with him.

While Michael continued talking about the wonders of the new security system, I was thinking about those voices coming from the bedroom. The talker was Carolyn, I was pretty sure of that. She didn't give me any hard evidence that she was the murderer, but she did talk about someone keeping their mouth shut and "proof." I still couldn't figure out who the mumbler was. Did I actually think it might have been Michael? Impossible. He was a nice guy and I had no reason to suspect him. Any guy who liked me couldn't be all bad. Besides, he was too gorgeous to be a crook.

"Are you ready to go? You don't seem too interested in hearing about my work."

I tuned back in. "I'm interested; just getting hungry. I haven't eaten much today. And yes, I'm ready, but I did want to express my condolences to Mrs. Burns. Why don't you get our coats and I'll see if she's available?"

He agreed and went off in search of the butler.

I climbed upstairs, as fast as I could, intent upon checking Carolyn's bedroom. The door was opened slightly. There was no one else in sight and hopefully Mr. Stiff Upper Lip Butler was busy getting our coats.

I accidentally nudged the door with my foot. At least I hoped it looked accidental, in case anyone was watching. As I peeked around the corner, I gained confidence. After all, this wasn't a movie or TV. This was real life and no one would hurt me. George had assured me that my car wreck was an accident and the jury was still out on the gas leak. So I felt pretty safe.

The huge bedroom was too opulent for my taste. And almost as big as my carriage house. Off to the left was the bathroom. I didn't see or hear anyone, so I stepped inside.

The ornate and fussy furniture looked like it was lifted directly from Buckingham Palace. I smirked as I pictured Carolyn lounging on the brocade-covered furniture in an overly dramatic pose. The red velvet was cloying and I almost choked at the ostentatious décor of the room.

I took a few more steps inside. The room was obsessively neat. Mine would be neat too if I had the servants she had. There didn't appear to be anything out of the ordinary—at least for that house.

I opened the gigantic walk-in closet. My bedroom could easily fit in it. Women's clothing, shoes, hats, bags and general "stuff" filled the entire area. I wondered where Dr. Burns' clothes were. Surely Carolyn hadn't disposed of them already. I didn't see another closet, but perhaps he'd used one in another bedroom.

"Ms. Darling, may I help you?"

Carolyn Burns poked her head around the corner and seemed happy that she caught me off guard and red-handed.

"I was just looking for the bathroom. Is this the only one up here?"

"Come now, Ms. Darling. Isn't it just possible that you were snooping? Isn't that a bit rude? To be snooping through the bedroom of a grieving widow?"

I knew I was right. Carolyn Burns was a smart-alec. Maybe that wasn't incontrovertible evidence that she was a murderer, but it sure helped point the finger.

"I'm sorry you feel that way, Mrs. Burns. I wasn't snooping. I just have a lousy sense of direction." It was a clever line and it was delivered with no eye contact.

"Then I apologize. I'll be happy to show you to the other powder room."

"No need. I don't have to go anymore. So I think I'll go home. I have a date with Michael, you know." I couldn't pass up the opportunity to rub it in.

Carolyn looked uncomfortable and a mite jealous. Of course, I was delighted with that.

I exited, with a lot more aplomb than I felt. This woman made me sick—figuratively and literally. I felt so dizzy that I almost needed the use of her chaise lounge myself. These vibes of mine were a pain in the butt. They'd never been this bad before. Maybe that was because I'd never met a murderer before Carolyn. The room spun around every time I was near her and only slightly less so around Michael. It made no sense to me that I felt the same way around Michael as I did around Carolyn. There's no way he was involved in the crime; I just knew it. I wondered why I felt so unsteady around him.

Rather than dwell on that, I chose to ignore it and

concentrate on clearing my head. Despite telling Carolyn I didn't need the bathroom, I found it and did a mirror talk.

"Listen, Sam, don't be a wimp. You know Carolyn is the murderer because of your physical reaction toward her. Go with those instincts. Believe them. Now stop being a dizzy blonde." That made me laugh and I suddenly realized that I was making a lot of noise and quickly flushed the toilet, hoping that would cover my indiscretion.

"And yes, she's beautiful…but Michael likes you. She's just a business arrangement to him." I batted my baby blues at myself and felt more confident.

Well, enough introspection. It was time to let Michael follow me home and for us to finally go on our date.

Gus was already gone, so there was no one else I needed to speak to. I garnered my coat from Michael and we started out the door. I had the feeling I was forgetting something, but couldn't figure out what it was.

"Hi ya, Sam. Forget something?" George grinned.

I glowered. "Go get in the car."

I turned to the guy who mattered. "Michael, I need to drop George off at the church. That's where he left his car. I'll meet you at my house in about fifteen minutes. Okay?" My glower turned to a glow.

"Sure. See you in a few minutes. Bye, Detective. Good

to see you."

"Yeah, you too, O'Dear."

After Michael turned away George spoke again, "By the way, O'Dear, I'd like to get together with you tomorrow and talk about the case. I heard you tell Sam that Mrs. Burns hired you to protect her and also to investigate the murder. I want to hear what you know."

Michael turned back toward us. "Sure, Detective, I'd be happy to meet with you. Maybe you can help me too."

I really didn't want to talk to George during the trip back to the parking lot, but I wanted to get information from him. Short of giving him mind-altering drugs, the only way I could milk his brain was to talk to him.

"So, George," I turned and smiled, "did you find out anything?"

"WATCH OUT!"

I swerved, missing the car in front of us by inches. My smile disappeared.

"So, did you find out anything?" My eyes were glued to the road; my hands gripped the steering wheel.

"I found out that Dr. and Mrs. Burns didn't share the master bedroom. He used one of the guest rooms."

"Oh, I knew that. His clothes weren't in the closet in the master suite." I didn't care that I sounded smug and self-satisfied.

"So what were you doing in Carolyn's bedroom?"

"Using the bathroom," I lied, not hard to do with my eyes on the road. "What else did you find out?"

"He had a sweetie on the side."

"Everybody knows that. Gwen Schneider."

"Nah, I mean besides her."

I turned my head and stared at him. I didn't want him to see my surprise—or get in a wreck—so I quickly faced forward again. Maybe I needed to delve a little more at work tomorrow.

"Who's the other girlfriend?" I tried to sound nonchalant.

"I don't know, but apparently she's fairly new."

"Okay, I'll find out for you, if you want." I stopped the rental next to his unmarked police car.

"Sure, yeah. Well, here we are. Don't forget, Sam. We'll talk more at dinner tomorrow night. I'll see you at six at The Rectory." George opened the door.

"I won't forget. You'll recognize me as the one wearing a bunny fur and wrist corsage."

"Very funny. Thanks for the ride. I'll see you tomorrow."

After he shut the car door I thought that George was the last person I wanted to concentrate on right now, but his face kept popping up in my brain as I drove away. I wondered why he was being so nice to me. I also wondered what he wanted. The good news was that he said it was okay for me to find out who Dr. Burns' new girlfriend was. For now though, I needed to just forget about good old George Lansing as I had other fish to fry.

I wished I had time to bait the hook a little better, but Michael was already parked by the carriage house when I pulled up.

"Hi." His smile lit up his face and my hopes.

"Hi. Come on in. I need just a minute to freshen up." Was that me who said "freshen up?" I'd never said those words before in my life. "I also have to take Clancy out for a few minutes."

Clancy vacillated between being happy to see me and glaring at me because I'd been gone for the day. She gave in and got excited. When she wagged her tail, her whole butt moved from side to side in what I called the "Clancy Rumba." It was cute and endearing, making me remember another reason we adopted her.

"Nice dog," Michael said as he hunkered down with his palm outstretched.

"Thanks. She's a member of the family."

Clancy sidled over to Michael and began sniffing him. Finally she lay down in front of him and rolled onto her back, allowing him to scratch her belly.

I laughed, "I'm afraid she has no shame."

"That's all right with me," Michael replied, "I love dogs."

"Would you like a drink while you're waiting? I'm afraid all I have is beer and wine."

"I'll take a beer. Why don't you do what you have to do and I'll help myself."

He and Clancy were still involved when I left the room.

It only took me a moment to "freshen up." I decided to wear the same outfit I'd worn all day and only needed to refresh my make up and run a brush through my hair.

By the time I returned, Michael was sitting on the couch drinking a beer and Clancy was sitting in front of him with a look of adoration on her face.

"C'mon, girl. Let's go outside."

She beat me to the door. I heard Michael laugh at her behavior. That made me like him even more.

Clancy didn't need a leash to go outside. She was trained to stay in the yard. She also was trained to "use the facilities" on all of Georgianne's plants. An immature move on my part, I knew, but by the time I thought better of it, it was too late to change Clancy's behavior. Since it was January, Clancy's choices were limited and she chose a small evergreen by Georgianne's back door.

I filled Clancy in on the latest goings on while we were outside, hoping that this would appease her a bit. She appeared interested but I could tell that she thought she should be my crime-solving partner rather than Michael or Gus.

Clancy finished her business and looked at me expectantly. "Good girl, Clancy. C'mon, let's go in."

She wasn't excited about returning inside and I finally pushed her a little with my knee, urging her through the door. She looked at me, sniffed, glanced at Michael once, turned on the charm to get one more scratch from him, and then went to her bed. I used to think it was my bed, but actually we shared it. However, I was sure that Clancy thought it was hers and that she allowed me to share it with her.

"Okay. I'm ready."

"You look great."

Hating the flush I felt on my cheeks, I said, "I'm wearing the same thing I had on earlier."

"You looked great earlier too."

I smiled as we put on our coats. It seemed I was smiling a lot tonight.

"If it's all right with you," Michael said, "I'd like to get the business done first. Then we can enjoy our meal and our date."

I agreed that it was a good idea.

We drove in a companionable silence for the few blocks to The Rectory. One of the downsides of living in a small town is that the dining choices are limited. So I'd be here two nights in a row, with two different guys. I definitely thought it was cool, even if one of them was George.

As we walked the half block from the parking lot to the restaurant door, Michael took my hand and said, "There are some things I want to clear up with you. You wanted to know what I was doing at Burns' office, what I was doing in the ER the night Charlie Schneider was acting up, and about my relationship with Carolyn Burns."

My mouth dropped open. Not only was he holding my hand in public, Michael was going to answer my every question, and maybe at some point he might answer my every need. I could hope anyway.

Nonchalantly, I replied, "If you really want to tell me all that, I guess I can listen."

"Please don't play dumb. I like it much better when you are yourself. You are one smart lady, and I like that."

The guy was gorgeous, he was kind, and he wanted to tell me everything I wanted to know. So I guess it was time for me to get dizzy.

THIRTEEN

"SORRY, MICHAEL." I wobbled. "I'm feeling a little woozy. Maybe I need some food."

"Well, just to be safe, I'll make sure we get a small table and I'll sit close so I can catch you if you fall." He smiled. I thought he was kidding, but wasn't quite sure.

Michael pulled open the Rectory's large oak door with stained glass inserts and stepped aside so I could enter first.

"Sam, welcome. It is so good to see you." Anthony, the owner, hugged me so tightly I could barely breathe. His hearty laugh reverberated throughout my body. "And who is this young man with you?"

"Anthony, this is Michael O'Dear, he's new in town." I disentangled myself from my friend. "And Michael, this is Anthony Lasorda. He owns The Rectory and don't ask him if he's related to the former Los Angeles Dodgers' coach. He'll talk all night."

They exchanged pleasantries as Anthony escorted us to a much-coveted table. He then kept us busy with a run down of his large family. This one started college, that one got married, this one joined the army. I never could keep up with his kids' names. It was difficult enough keeping track of my own family.

Finally we were settled, and, after gaining my assurance that I liked it, Michael ordered a bottle of California merlot.

Anthony beamed. "An excellent choice, Mr. O'Dear. If you permit, I will make a special meal for you. It's not on the menu, but you will love it. Are you a vegetarian like Sam or may I put some seafood in your portion?"

Michael admitted he was a practicing carnivore and that any kind of meat or fish would be fine with him. This was the first and only strike against him.

Anthony left to personally prepare our dinners and Michael turned his attention to me. "We said we'd get business out of the way. Are you ready to talk?"

Was I ever. "Sure." It was hard acting nonchalant.

Michael began, "I was at the clinic because I was meeting with Burns. He'd hired me after clinic employees complained someone had been rifling through the patient files in his office. Things were out of place. Nothing had been taken as far as anyone could tell, but things had been disturbed. A file clerk was the first one to notice and mentioned it to Burns. When it happened a few more times, he brought me in. He claimed he wasn't concerned about it though." Almost as an afterthought, he added, "Also some patients were threatening to sue him over alleged improprieties."

"What were they?"

He looked adorable as he refused my request. "You know I can't tell you that. Therapists aren't the only ones bound by confidentiality. Anyway, I took the job and found it only mildly interesting." He almost absentmindedly fiddled with his silverware. "I hadn't really gotten into it much before Burns was killed. So that's why I was at the clinic."

"Okay, I buy that. But why were you at the ER in the middle of the night?"

"I was there because of Charlie Schneider. I told you Mrs. Burns wanted me to do some investigating about the murder." He broke off a piece of Italian bread and buttered it. "I'd heard from some former employees that Burns and Gwen Schneider had been involved in a long-term affair and I was checking her out as a possible suspect. Her brother was a real loose cannon. Half crazy. Burns had told me he was seeing Charlie as a patient as a favor to Gwen. I was following him that night and got to the ER waiting room just in time to knock the gun out of his hand. By the way, I convinced the DA not to prosecute. He's already on probation for some minor offenses, and they're just going to continue supervision, as long as he continues therapy with someone. Charlie's a sad case. He lost his wife and kid at that hospital and has never been the same."

"So far, so good. Now what is the real relationship between you and Carolyn Burns?" I waited expectantly, hoping that he'd give the answer I wanted.

"It's exactly what I told you. She hired me because the murderer is still on the loose and she felt the need for a bodyguard. That's it. She doesn't mean anything to me. I mean, it's kind of cool to have a famous novelist in Quincy. So I've been having fun with it."

I looked at him.

"Close your mouth. It's true. And that's that. Now I'd like to hear what you know. Fair is fair."

I figured I'd better tell him what I knew so we could get to the important stuff, like our date.

Anthony returned with the wine, let Michael sniff and swirl, and poured our glasses full after Michael nodded approval. After we clinked glasses and each took a drink, I answered Michael's question. "I don't really know much. I know that Gwen Schneider and Charlie Schneider did not kill Burns. Charlie confessed to try to save his sister. I don't know why Gwen confessed, but she didn't do it. I'm positive of that."

"I'm probably going to be sorry I asked, but how do you know that Gwen didn't do it?"

I ignored his smart comment, because I was ready to fall in love with him. "Okay, I'll tell you. She doesn't *feel* guilty. Before you start laughing at me, I gotta tell you something about me. See, sometimes I feel things; I get vibes about people. And sometimes I'm right and sometimes I'm wrong, but most of the time I'm right. And I'm 100% sure on this one. Just like I'm 100% sure that Carolyn killed her husband."

"Sounds like you've been reading Carolyn's thrillers."

Once again, I ignored his smart-ass comment. Did he realize just what I was going through to show my interest in him?

"She just *feels* guilty, Michael. In fact, the feeling is so powerful that I get dizzy or sick whenever I'm around her. And it's not the flu or an upset stomach. She literally makes me sick. I cannot stand to be around her. She's evil."

My intense feelings about the woman propelled me into a standing position. My hands were flat on the table and I loomed over Michael.

Michael looked directly into my eyes as he said, "I just don't buy it. I mean, I think you believe it, but I'm not into that stuff."

"I'm not into that stuff either. This is just part of who I am. I've always been this way. Even when I was a little kid I'd get these feelings about people and I'd get twitches and stuff all over my body."

"Twitches?" He tried and failed to suppress a disbelieving grin.

"Yeah, twitches." I sat. "And sometimes dizziness and other times just feelings, just vibrations." I found it hard to explain this to anyone, especially this gorgeous hunk who would now never touch me except to push me away.

He hesitated, then spoke softly, "You get dizzy around me too."

I put my hand on his, then quickly withdrew it. "What I feel around Carolyn is nothing like what I feel around you. I promise."

He relaxed against the back of his chair.

I continued. "I know it sounds crazy. That's why I haven't told many people. I'm telling you because I need you to believe me. Carolyn killed her husband. No ifs, ands, or buts. She did it. Period. End of quote."

"Okay, let's say you're right."

I smiled.

"This is just for argument's sake. Let's say you're right. How in the world could the police arrest Carolyn for her husband's murder without any evidence?"

"Aw, come on, Michael. Cops arrest people without evidence all the time. Don't you watch television? Anyway, what we need to do is find the evidence and then we can turn it over to my brother, Rob, who will notify Detective Lansing and then Rob will be promoted. I'll be vindicated. And you…" I hesitated.

"And I'll what?"

"And you'll believe me." Gee, I almost slipped up there and said, "…you'll fall in love with me." Where did I get this crap? I hadn't felt like this in more years than I cared to remember.

"What did Gwen Schneider say when you asked her why she confessed?"

"What?" I practically stuttered.

He began to repeat his question, "What did Gwen—"

I interrupted, "I heard you. I said 'what' because I can't believe I've not asked her why she confessed. In the beginning everything was moving so quickly and then she was arrested and was in jail. I just didn't think of it."

Michael spoke softly, "See, Sam. You're a social worker, not a cop."

I ignored his statement and continued, "Will you help me?" I tried not to beg.

"Under one condition. That you let me do it. It's my job. You're a social worker, not a cop, not a private investigator. A social worker."

Same song, different singer. Ho-hum. "Okay. I'll stay out of it." I carefully avoided eye contact. Gee, this lying and not looking people in the eye was a lot easier than I had anticipated.

"Let's change the subject, and talk about you," Michael said.

"And you," I added.

I noticed that "you" and "you" didn't add up to a "we," but that only meant it was our first real date. "We" could become a reality.

The rest of the all-too-short evening was delightful. Michael asked all the right questions about me, my kids, marriage, and family. Since I'm a therapist, I asked open-ended questions. He rewarded me with rich conversation.

No, he'd never been married. Been close a few times. Yes, he moved here recently, liked Quincy, and would like to stay for a while. Born and raised in St. Louis. He learned his skills as a military policeman in the Army. No, he'd never met Carolyn Burns before her husband's murder. She'd found his name in the yellow pages and didn't know beforehand that he'd worked for her husband.

Okay, those aren't the responses to open-ended questions. Maybe I did interrogate him a little, but I was entitled. I'd waited a long time for a real date, and getting together with Michael had proven to be very problematic. Finally, my equilibrium had stabilized, my hair was behaving, and even my mouth was cooperating. Not much cussing tonight.

Then, in a gesture I was eagerly anticipating, Michael

touched my hand and leaned toward me. As he did so, I wondered if we were having an earthquake. My balance was disrupted. I nearly fell off my chair, but two strong arms caught me and kept me vertical.

"We need to get you home, Sam."

"No, I'm fine." This time I whined.

"I'm not going to argue with you. It's home and to bed."

He meant alone.

FOURTEEN

"…AS HE APPROACHED me, I fancied he had ideas about my virtue. His eyes were heated, as was my body. I waited for him to speak, but no words escaped his lips. He merely touched my bodice, and delicately undid the top button, being very careful not to touch the skin underneath. I feared I would swoon, but did not. Instead I looked at him with eyes that were as lustful as his own. A sigh escaped my lips and I…"

DING!

Thank God. It was over. Listening to Mrs. Abernathy was like reading a steamy romance novel.

"Mrs. Abernathy, I'm sorry. Your time is up for this session."

"Oh no, Ms. Darling. I was just getting to the interesting part of my dream. Couldn't we just stretch the time a bit so I can describe the rest? I know you will be able to appreciate it." Her bottom lip quivered as her chest heaved. My heart was palpitating a bit as well. Mrs. Abernathy did a wonderful job of describing her dream.

It was amazing that her dreams were so sexual and so vivid. She was a short, rotund, elderly woman wearing a conservative black frock, and she was homely. That was the kindest adjective I could summon to describe her. Her dreams, however, were erotic enough for the letters section of a porn magazine.

"I'm sorry, Mrs. Abernathy. Your time is up for this session." I learned the broken record routine years ago in a not-needed assertive training class. "We can continue next week. Make sure you confirm your appointment with Mrs. Schmitt at the front desk. Good-bye and have a wonderful week."

"But, Ms. Darling…"

I stood and assisted Mrs. Abernathy to the door. "I look forward to talking to you again next week."

"All right. Perhaps I'll write down my dreams during the week to make sure I won't forget any of them." She had a hopeful look in her eye.

"Certainly. That will be fine. 'Bye." Oh, joy. I'd have to listen to her dreams for another hour.

My first patient at my new job. What a disappointment. I had visions of helping people sort out real difficulties in their lives. Instead I got Mrs. Abernathy. I no longer wondered why Marian and the others had grinned at the staff meeting when I received Mrs. Abernathy as my first client. I guessed that she had already been a part of their caseloads and had been passed from person to person.

I could empathize with Mrs. Abernathy because I wanted to note on her chart, Diagnosis: Lonely, Bored and Horny. While I was trying to do a diagnostic interview, she spent the hour energetically describing the erotic dreams she'd been having. When I got to know her better, perhaps I would recommend she try writing romance novels. She might be quite successful.

That reminded me of Carolyn Burns. I was more convinced than ever that she killed Dr. Burns. Unfortunately, my "vibes" wouldn't stand up in court, and I really didn't want to talk about my instincts publicly. It was bad enough that some of my sibs knew. They'd stopped teasing me about it years ago, but most weren't comfortable talking about my gift/curse. Now Michael knew and soon others would find out. This could prove to be embarrassing.

I just had to find some hard evidence.

As I went through the private door from my office to the kitchen, I noticed the closed door on the other side of that large room. It led to Burns' office, which was still off limits to us. "The investigation is ongoing," the press release stated. It was posted all over the office so I couldn't pretend I didn't know.

Since my office connected to the kitchen and the

kitchen connected to the scene of the crime, I could slip into Burns' office without anyone knowing. And I wouldn't even feel guilty about it.

I tiptoed across the kitchen. Maybe I wasn't going to feel guilty but I still needed to be discreet.

The door was closed. I crossed my fingers and gently turned the knob. That was impossible to do with my fingers crossed. I uncrossed my fingers and quietly opened the door a few inches and peeked inside. No one there. And the door leading from his office to the hallway was closed.

Before anyone could come into the kitchen and interrupt my sleuthing, I moved quickly into Burns' office and closed the door. The room looked just as it had the last time I was in it, with two notable exceptions. First, there was no dead body on the floor. Second, standing in the corner, rifling through a file cabinet, was none other than Carolyn Burns.

Intent on her evil deeds, she didn't notice me until I spoke.

"So, Carolyn. It's curtains for you."

"I beg your pardon." Even though I caught her in the act, she did a great job of making me feel inept and in the wrong.

"It's curtains for you. You're up a creek without a paddle. You're S.O.L. You know. You returned to the scene of the crime. I caught you."

"Ms. Darling, even though you are speaking in clichés, I have no idea what you are talking about. I have every right to be in my husband's office."

"Not when there's masking tape or scotch tape or something barring the door."

"I wondered if you'd noticed that, Ms. Darling. So what are you doing here?"

Okay, she had me there. "That's none of your concern. There was no tape over the door I used and besides, I just caught you snooping through those confidential files."

This all fit. Burns had hired Michael because someone had been going through his files. I now knew who that someone was. Finally, I was getting the much-needed evidence and the noose was tightening around Carolyn's neck. Well, maybe that was a little melodramatic, but it expressed my sentiments succinctly.

"I was looking for some insurance papers and I notified the new receptionist that I was doing so. Any other questions?" She looked so smug and self-righteous that I wanted to smack her. That would certainly wipe the grin off her face.

"You're looking for insurance papers in the patient file drawer?" Aha, I had her now.

"Oh, no wonder I couldn't find them. I thought this

file cabinet was where my husband kept his personal files." How she managed to look so innocent was beyond me.

"All right, Carolyn. I'll check with Mrs. Schmitt in just a moment. In the meantime, I'll notify Officer Darling that you are here."

She merely raised an eyebrow. I guess my brother Rob wasn't enough of a threat.

"And I will also notify Detective Lansing."

"There's no need to do that, Ms. Darling." I found the lever that could move her. "I was just leaving and you can see that I have nothing in my hands."

She had a big purse however. "I'm sorry, Carolyn, but I feel obligated to tell the authorities. I'm sure you understand."

"Why must you do that?" Then she did what many heroines in her books did when they got upset. She sat down and cried. That was the only part of her characterizations I didn't like. It was hard admitting that everything else about her books intrigued me. In fact, they seemed familiar to me and contained good descriptions of people's neuroses and psychoses.

I continued the conversation while slowly advancing toward her. "I already told you when I was at your house. I know you killed your husband. And I also know you had help."

"It's not true." She paused and looked up at me. "How do you know all that?"

It was time for me to sing the same song again. "I just know." I didn't want to tell her how I knew and I also didn't want to tell her that I knew she was too prissy to actually stick the scalpel in his neck.

"Just like you know Gwen Schneider didn't do it?"

"Where did you hear that?"

"You're not the only one Michael talks to." Her smile made me want to pass out. That was just a figure of speech. Oddly enough, this time I didn't feel faint around her. Maybe my anger helped control my dizziness.

For good measure I threw in, "And you cut the gas line in my house and the brake line in my car."

"We did not cut the brake line in your car. That's ludicrous."

I pounced. "You said 'we.'"

She turned away. "I meant 'I.'"

I took another step toward her. "So you admit you tampered with the gas line in my home."

She sighed as she faced me again. "That is so patently ridiculous it doesn't even deserve comment."

"Well, you have fingerprint powder all over your nice black suit." I guess I showed her. I resisted the urge to stick out my tongue and go "nyah-nyah-nyah."

She wiped at the grayish-white powder. Her fingers

beat a staccato tattoo on her thighs. She accompanied the beat with "ooh-ooh, ooh-ooh." What a priss.

She was fastidious all right. I wondered if she was around when the blood started spurting from her husband's neck like a full-speed-ahead garden hose. How did she handle that?

As I thought about that gory detail, the door from the hallway opened and a familiar voice announced his presence, "Hi ya, Sam. Mrs. Burns."

"George, I was just about to call you. Carolyn is in here without permission." Oh my God. I'd turned into the very person I despised—a tattletale. This was gross. "And she's going through the file cabinets. Make her stop." I was talking and I couldn't shut up.

George looked quizzically at me, then shook his head as if to clear it of my face. "Mrs. Burns, I've been looking for you. Saw your car outside. Will you please accompany me to the station so we can talk?"

"Does she need a lawyer? Are you going to read her her rights?" I was as excited as a girl on her first date.

He didn't spare a glance in my direction. He was good at this.

"Of course, Officer Lansing. I'll be happy to oblige. Will I need to notify my attorney?"

"We just want to talk. You aren't under arrest. Of course, if you want to have your attorney present, you may. By the way, I understood that O'Dear was providing security service for you. Where is he?"

"Waiting at my home, I presume. I needed some, um, private time, so I left by a side door. These insurance papers are very important to me and I felt I couldn't wait until you declared this area open again. I'm certainly sorry if I broke any rules."

I didn't buy what she was selling. Like I thought she was really sorry. I understood her quite well and predicted that the next thing she would do was bat her eyes.

Gosh almighty, if she didn't. She batted her eyes at George, and I could tell he liked it. The scum-sucking dog.

"Mrs. Burns, we'll talk about what you're doing here later. For now, let's go to the station. I have some other questions for you."

Carolyn gathered her belongings and wiggled out the door.

I couldn't resist one last jab at her. "Look in her purse. Bet she's got something in there that she shouldn't have."

"Bye, Sam. See ya tonight."

Oh, yeah, tonight. I'd almost forgotten. A dinner with George. I hesitated to call it a dinner date, because it wasn't a date, not a real one. He'd had his chance at a date with me back in the '80s. And he blew it. Big time.

One strike and you are out, George Lansing.

He poked his balding head back through the door. "And, Sam. Please leave this room. Now. And I'd appreciate it if you didn't return until we've cleared it. Got that?"

"I understand." I understood, but that didn't mean I was going to do what he said.

As he slithered out the hall door, I exited through the kitchen and snagged a cup of coffee on the way to my office.

I sat in my chair, plopped my feet on the desk, and wrapped both hands around the mug. There's something comforting about the warmth of a mug of coffee. So why didn't I feel comforted?

Why didn't anyone believe me about Carolyn Burns? At least Michael claimed he wanted to believe me. That was a giant leap ahead of George, who just looked at me with that condescending grin of his and sloughed me off as if I were a child. I wondered if my brother Rob had any other information about the case. I also wondered if he would share it with me.

A quick call to the Quincy Police Department told me that Rob was out on patrol. I didn't leave a message.

I took a big swig of the dark rich brew. My next step needed careful planning. Would there be any value in checking Burns' files? Would I know if something were missing?

I wished I could figure out who was in on this with Carolyn. The only people I was sure were innocent were Gwen and Charlie Schneider. Everyone else was up for grabs.

And why did Burns tell Michael he wasn't concerned about the patient files being out of order? Did he think it was the result of carelessness? Or was it something more sinister; was Burns himself involved?

There was something else niggling at my brain. Every time it tried to surface I pushed it back down. I didn't want to think about it. But these few minutes alone were all it needed to rear its ugly head.

Michael. Dear, sweet, handsome, nice butt, Michael. Would I care to examine that I got dizzy almost every time I was around him? Would I care to compare faintness with the times that I was around Carolyn? Both felt the same. The loss of balance was certainly the same.

The first time I had seen Carolyn was at her house on the day after her husband was murdered. She and Michael were talking together. And I felt dizzy. They both touched me and I passed out. As I was getting up from the chaise lounge, they both touched me again. Dizziness again. That had to be a coincidence. Michael and Carolyn were not accomplices in murder. I was sure of that.

Devil Sam: "Just a coincidence. Michael had nothing to do with the murder."

Angel Sam: "You've been dizzy more around Michael than you've ever been around Carolyn. At least look at the possibility that he's involved."

Devil Sam: "Don't bother. He's much too cute to have murdered anyone. Besides it's been more years than you care to remember since you have…you know…had sex."

I had to stop those schizophrenic meanderings. Anyway, Devil Sam must not be too good at what she does if she has such a hard time talking about sex. I didn't think I was the type of morally bankrupt person who would let the possibility of getting laid get in the way of justice.

To distract myself, I decided to catch up on reading some of my professional journals and quit thinking about the case. A boring, but necessary, part of being a therapist is keeping up with the latest research. I couldn't say how much time passed before I heard someone knock hesitantly on the door and open it just a crack.

I looked up to see two well-matched heads peeking around the doorframe. "Gwen. Charlie. Come on in. When did they spring you?" I couldn't believe what I heard myself saying. I sounded like a cop.

"Hi Sam," Gwen said. "They had a preliminary

hearing this morning and the judge didn't find enough evidence to bind me over for trial."

She motioned her brother to come into the room so she could close the door. "Officer Lansing couldn't hear everything from the other room — he only heard part of what I said to you. And since you're a therapist, bound by confidentiality, my lawyer made a good case for them not pressing charges against me. He said I could still be picked up again, but I'm free for now."

"Good for you. That serves Officer Lansing right. Eavesdropping is a nasty habit." Surprisingly enough, I was able to say that with a straight face. I was sure glad I didn't have to testify. It would have sounded nuts for me to say that Gwen was innocent because she didn't "feel" guilty.

"I just came by to get my stuff. Under the circumstances, I figured that I shouldn't be working here. Anyway, I thought I'd leave before they fired me." The sniffling began again. Luckily Brother Charlie was quick with a handkerchief.

I thought this was an opportune time to get the skinny on Gwen's relationship with Burns. "Charlie, would you mind sitting in the waiting room for a little while? I'd like to talk to your sister privately."

He exited without objection. His hangdog expression left a pall in the room as he walked out.

"Why did you confess to me?" I wasn't going to forget to ask this again.

She seemed surprised by my question. "I don't know. I think I was in shock. It was really stupid to say it. Now you and Charlie are the only ones who believe I'm innocent."

I decided to continue the direct approach. "Is it true you were having an affair with Dr. Burns?"

Niagara Falls began. "Yes," snort, slobber, "but he broke it off with me about a month before he died."

Gwen had a real talent for shutting those waterworks on and off. I held my suspicions at bay but knew that she wasn't being entirely straight with me.

"Gwen, is there anything I can do to help you now?" I reached out and put my hand on her arm. No dizziness on my part.

"No, I've got to sort it out by myself. But..." she looked at the connecting door to the kitchen.

"Is something else bothering you?"

She said, "No," but her eyes kept straying to the door.

I got up and checked, pulling the door toward me. The kitchen was empty. "Nobody there this time."

Then she really started blubbering. "I really didn't mean to, but I did and I'm sorry and Dr. Burns..." More slobbering and more mumbling and not much clear conversation, but her glance kept straying toward the kitchen door.

"Gwen, I can't understand what you are saying. Can you please calm down and tell me what you did and what you are sorry for?" I was getting tired of these half-confessions.

This was getting more and more curious. Why did Gwen insist on confessing to me all the time when I knew she was innocent?

She regained some composure. "Charlie said that you fed him and helped him when I was in jail. I don't know what's gonna happen to him if I leave or if they..." Slobber, slobber, etc.

She really collapsed then and I couldn't get a coherent word out of her. She still couldn't keep her eyes away from the door leading to the kitchen. In between hiccups and blubbering, that is. So acting on a hunch, I got up quietly, opened the kitchen door, walked through that room, and quickly and with lots of force opened the door to Burns' office. A loud thump produced a grunt of satisfaction in me. The thump was the result of Carolyn Burns landing ignominiously on her butt. She lay spread-eagle on the floor. I was sure the position was not unknown to her. The look on her face was worth anything I might have to experience.

The look on her face said, "Guilty as charged."

FIFTEEN

FROM HER NEW position on the floor, Carolyn grunted her displeasure. I felt a bump behind me as Gwen moved close to look over my shoulder. I tried to behave professionally, since I was on duty and since we were in the office of the dearly departed. I tried, but I failed. The laughter escaped. It felt wonderful to cut loose with a belly laugh. I laughed so hard tears streamed down my face. I laughed so hard I snorted. I laughed so hard I couldn't see. I laughed so hard I couldn't breathe. I laughed so hard that Carolyn and Gwen left without me noticing.

I wondered why they left together, when they should actually hate each other. Maybe it was just a coincidence. Tears were still overflowing from my bout of uncontrollable mirth when I went out to the waiting room to see if Charlie was still there.

"Clara, did you see Charlie Schneider leave?"

"Are you all right?"

"I'm fine." Snort. "Allergies." Hiccup. "Did you see

Charlie leave?"

"Yes, he went out rather quickly after Gwen and Mrs. Burns."

"Are you sure they left together or was it just accidental that they went out the door at the same time?"

"I'm quite sure they left together. They were speaking to one another as they left." Even though Clara Schmitt was brand new, she didn't miss a trick. She looked deceptively like a grandmother type, but this lady was sharp. If she said they left together, I guess I needed to believe her.

I didn't call George or Rob, since I'd see George in a few hours. There was only one person on my caseload because of the confusion after the funeral, so I decided to take off early, go home and relax before my dinner with George.

I had walked to work today. The frigid crispness of the January day was just what I'd needed to uncloud my mind. Walking home was even better. The late afternoon sun danced over the ice and snow and brought fanciful notions to my head. I imagined that I was an owner of one of the mansions instead of just a renter. The thought made me walk taller. This was a great neighborhood.

Clancy was waiting at the door for me. Leash in mouth.

"Gee, Clance, can't you give me one minute before we

go for a walk?"

The answer was "No." It was comforting to have her in my life, but I could understand why she was upset. Normally we spent a lot of time together, but with my accidents and two dates in a row, it's no wonder she was feeling left out.

I thought about calling Pete, but he had told me he was working evenings this week. The rest of the tribe would be busy at this hour, coming home from work and spending a little time with their families before dinner. I didn't want to disturb anyone just to run my ideas by them. Maybe Clancy would suffice. She was my best bet anyway, at least until I could talk to George or Michael. It seemed like a good idea to solidify my thoughts before I tried to talk to either one of them. Neither was convinced that I knew what I was talking about. And Clancy didn't think I was crazy—at least she didn't tell me so.

"Okay, let's go. I guess I could use the exercise myself. I need to talk about some stuff too. Maybe you could help me." I threw my purse on the couch and opened the door, letting Clancy lead the way. She took off for her favorite haunts with me dutifully following at leash length.

"I'm positive Carolyn killed her husband. But I'm also sure she had help. She's much too prissy to stick a scalpel into someone. Now who was her accomplice?"

Clancy turned and looked at me thoughtfully. She cocked her head in her thinking mode, but didn't say anything. *Gosh, Sam, of course she didn't say anything, you nitwit. She's a dog.*

"Here's the list of possibles. Gwen Schneider. I know she didn't do it, because she feels innocent. She sure acts strange though. But that's no reason to consider her a murderer. Just because she semi-confessed to me twice doesn't mean she did it. Also, she and Carolyn certainly wouldn't be accomplices in this kind of thing. I do wonder why they left the clinic together though.

"Charlie Schneider. I think he just loves his sister a lot and relies on her to keep him almost sane. He doesn't feel guilty to me either, even though he confessed. He does have a motive though. He feels protective of his sister—she's the only family he has."

"Michael O'Dear. I know, Clance. He can't be guilty. He's too cute and he likes me. The only reason he's on the list is that I'm dizzy when I'm around him, the same as when I'm near Carolyn. So that's the list. I'm sure there are other possibilities. I mean, there's gotta be. Those three are all innocent. So we gotta find Carolyn's accomplice. Or maybe find out more about her. I mean, I could be wrong about her not being able to stick the scalpel in Burns. Maybe she used to be a surgical nurse, or a knife thrower in a circus or something."

Or maybe she's a psychopath. I didn't express that notion aloud; afraid that even Clancy would think it was too much.

On that note, we arrived at the park. I let Clancy off the leash for a while so she could run and tire herself out. I didn't feel like running. All of this brainwork was tiring. When Clancy came back to me with her tongue hanging out, we headed for home.

The return to our place passed quickly, with Clancy and me taking turns leading.

When we arrived, Clancy went to her corner, got a drink of water, and circled around for a nap.

It was time to decide on the all-important outfit. I climbed into my closet to begin the familiar ritual. What to wear. It was only George, so I grabbed a pair of jeans and a sweatshirt.

As I put them on I let Clancy in on my thoughts, "If I wear these clothes, he probably won't be consumed with desire for me, and then I wouldn't have so much fun being cold to him. So perhaps I ought to dress up a bit more." I looked over my shoulder for her opinion. She agreed.

There really wasn't much of a choice. I had already worn my power suit several times. Last night I wore my black cocktail dress with the black blazer. I had a brainstorm. Maybe jeans, a black camisole and the black blazer. Yes. Cool, sophisticated, and with just a hint of animal magnetism. I didn't want to bowl the poor guy over after all.

It was a clear, crisp night, so I put on some snow boots, placed my shoes in my large purse, found my "good" coat and bade farewell to Clancy.

"Clancy, old girl, watch and learn. I've had two dates in a row, with two different men. This is something you may never see again in either of our lifetimes." She raised her head and I swore she rolled her eyes. "Okay, don't look at me like that. I know the dinner with George isn't really a date, but it'll look that way to anyone who is watching, so it will still count. Give me a break."

I walked slowly to The Rectory, deliberately arriving twenty minutes late so George would be forced to wait for me. Anthony greeted me effusively at the door.

"Sam, what a pleasure. Two nights in a row. Are you meeting someone?"

"Yes, but I don't see him. Is Detective Lansing here?"

"No, but I do have a reservation in his name for two. Why don't I seat you and I'll stay on the lookout for him?"

"Okay, Anthony. And bring me a—"

"Beer in a long neck bottle, no glass." He chuckled. "Sam, you've been coming in here for a long time. I know what you drink by now."

This felt wonderful. I thought I only moved back to Quincy for the support of my family after my divorce. But I also moved back for this. People who have known me since I was born. People who care about me. There was comfort in being served by a man who knew that I sometimes had wine with dinner, but otherwise it was always beer in a long necked bottle. No glass. Did he suspect the phallic connotations?

The beer arrived quickly. I exchanged my boots for shoes, then I sipped and looked around. The Rectory always had a nice crowd. Some people came for a meal. Some people came for drinks. Some came to ease the loneliness a bit. All came to be catered to by Anthony—a great bear of a man with a heart that filled his entire body.

My mind stayed occupied, just looking around and saying "hello" every now and then to acquaintances. No relatives here tonight.

I finished my beer before I thought to look at my watch. I'd been here over twenty minutes. And that damn George wasn't here. He stood me up again. He did the same damn thing that he did in high school. This was stupid and I was steaming. I slammed some money on the table for the drink. I wouldn't stiff Anthony even though I'd been shafted.

Just as I stood up to get my coat, my glance caught the smiling face of The Late One.

I didn't reciprocate with a smile of my own. "What are you grinning at?"

"I'm happy to see ya, Sam. Why shouldn't I be smiling?"

"You think it's funny that you could stand me up again? You think it's funny that I'm waiting here and you didn't call?"

His smile disappeared, replaced by a frustrated frown and a furrowed brow. "Did you check your voice mail? Did you check your e-mail? I left a message on both since I was gonna be late and I didn't want you thinking I was standing you up."

Feeling stupid was not something I relished, but I did it well. "Sorry, I didn't check. I just assumed."

He resumed his original smiling expression. "I recall you've always done a lot of assuming. We used to say that you'd die by committing 'assumicide.' Why, I remember the time when we were juniors when you—"

I interrupted, "George, I'm not really interested in walking down memory lane with you. It's lonely there."

He looked uncomfortable. "Now that we're middle-aged…" he blanched at my stare, "Now that we're adults, don't you think it might be a good idea to get rid of that stiff-necked pride long enough to let me explain what happened on prom night?"

I lifted my empty bottle toward the bartender and ordered a second beer. Feeling magnanimous, I ordered one for George too. "Okay, explain away." I still wasn't going to forgive him. After all, I was the one who had been left all dressed up with no place to go. My friends had been solicitous, but that didn't relieve the pain of being left with my pink organza formal, bunny fur, and high hopes.

He looked me in the eye and without blinking he began. "I was excited about prom too. Don't talk." He lifted a hand in a stop signal. "Don't talk, Sam."

He stopped me in mid-breath. He knew me well, this old beau of mine.

"I know it's hard for you to sit and listen. Your specialty is interrupting me and putting words in my mouth." I opened my mouth but couldn't get a word out. "Don't talk."

Shutting up was hard for me. "Don't say 'don't talk' again or I'll explode. I promise I'll be quiet unless you order me to. If you give me a royal command to shut up, then I'm gonna talk. Deal?"

He smiled in spite of himself. "Deal. Now may I get on with my explanation?"

I nodded. And didn't talk.

"Okay. I was excited about the prom too. It's hard for

a guy to admit that at any age, but it was especially hard when I was seventeen. But prom was a big deal. Renting that tux, borrowing my dad's car, looking forward to some real making out at the all-night party."

I couldn't help myself. "You wouldn't have gotten to second base."

"I didn't care. Rounding first was enough for me." He grinned again and made me forget that I hated the ground he walked on.

He continued. "I was all set to walk out the door when the phone rang. It was my best friend, Cal. His car was stuck in the mud out on Columbus Road and he wanted me to pick him up. Remember that he lived way out in the country?"

"And…?" I arched my eyebrows. This had better be good.

"And he was my best friend and I was a little early, so I drove out there and found him. He was about twelve miles out of town. Now there are lots of houses out that way, but back then there was nothing, no lights, no houses, no phones, no nothing."

Nothing is what I said.

"His car didn't look like it was stuck too badly, so instead of just giving him a ride into town, we decided to try to push the car out of the mud. And don't roll your eyes at me, Sam Darling. We were kids. Maybe we didn't think it through very well, but it seemed like the right thing to do at the time."

I raised my hand. "May I speak, sir?"

"Skip the sarcasm. It doesn't become you. It might have been cute when you were a teenager. But, now..." He took my beer bottle that I'd been squeezing the life out of and took the last swig.

"Okay," I said, "this isn't about me, it's about you. So cut to the chase. You and Cal decided to push his car out and you probably fell and got all muddy. You are going to use that as a pathetic excuse for not picking me up for prom. Puh-leeze." The waiter delivered the beers just in time. I grabbed mine and took a big gulp.

"Do you want to hear the truth, or do you want to continue making the story fit your misguided notions of what happened? We can play it either way."

I stared at the ceiling. I stared at the floor. I stared at the condensation on my bottle of beer. Anywhere but at George. Just before I was going to break under the pressure, he spoke again.

"Okay, you were right. Don't speak. Yes, you were right. I fell in the mud and got my tux completely ruined. I was embarrassed beyond belief and didn't know how to deal with that."

"So you decided to wait twenty-five years to tell me this?"

"That night I was embarrassed and scared and I didn't know how to tell you. I felt so stupid and didn't have enough self-confidence to admit what I'd done. I swore Cal to secrecy. It was too late to rent another tux and I didn't even own a suit. The next day I called and your mom said you 'weren't accepting phone calls from anyone named George Lansing.' I called you every day for two weeks and you wouldn't talk to me. I came to your house, I wrote you letters, and finally, I admitted to myself that it was over. You were so angry that you wouldn't let me explain. Remember that I was a kid too. I made stupid choices, Sam, but so did you. You chose to stay mad all these years, when it could have been over the day after prom."

For a moment, I noticed the sweet guy I had known. I almost felt some sympathy for him, but I quashed it as it was developing in my heart. "Okay, now you told me. Are you happy?"

"Of course I'm not happy about it. You and I had a great time together all through school. That ended the night of prom. I've missed you as a friend. Now that you're back in town, maybe we can rekindle our friendship."

I wasn't going to be that easy, although I wasn't completely against his suggestion. "We'll see. Listen, I really want to talk about the crime. That's the only reason we got together tonight. So tell me what you know."

"You are such an incurable romantic." He tore off a piece of Italian bread and began picking it apart absentmindedly.

Yeah, yeah, funny, funny. "Tell me what you know."

"In a minute." He had a strange look on his face. I wished I could read his feeble male mind. "I'd like you to go first. This is an official police investigation and I can't tell you everything. I'll be glad to share what I can, but you go first."

Was this a trick, designed to find out what I knew without giving away anything? I had a few minutes to think as our food arrived. My favorite meal again, pasta primavera and a house salad. I changed to white wine with the meal, although another beer would have tasted good too. George drove me to drink and that was a fact.

"Okay, I'll tell you what I know, but you gotta promise that you'll tell me some stuff too. Promise?"

Mouth bulging with food, he nodded. I took that to mean he agreed, but with George you never knew.

"Here's the scoop. I already told you that Carolyn killed her husband. Well, you know today I found Carolyn Burns snooping through confidential files in her husband's office. She said she was looking for some insurance papers, but that file cabinet only contains patient folders. You came in and took her downtown, so I hope she told you the truth about what she was doing." I waited expectantly, but he was mum. Not being real comfortable with silence, I continued.

"What you don't know is that a little later I was talking to Gwen Schneider and her brother in my office. I had a feeling something was going on again and for some reason Gwen kept looking at the door, as if she knew something was happening on the other side. The upshot is that I opened the door to Burns' office, knocked Carolyn on her butt, and while I was laughing my head off, Carolyn, Charlie and Gwen left the scene."

He was surprised but not shocked. "Together?"

I nodded. "She came back to the clinic after you let her go from the station. She was snooping through the files again, I bet." I punctuated my accusations with my fork beating against the plate.

"Did you see her snooping again?"

"No, but I bet she was. Why else would she be there?"

"Did you ever think that she might be getting some of her husband's things from his office? Doesn't that make more sense than assuming she was snooping?" He scooped another mouthful of pasta onto his fork.

"Remember I told you that during my initial interview Burns got a phone call. I don't know who he was talking to, but he got really angry and said something about having something for the person next week. He also said

'Leave me alone or you'll be sorry.' Maybe he was talking to Carolyn."

George took a drink of beer before responding. "Maybe he was talking to Fred Flintstone."

I didn't get caught up in his sarcasm. "George, she did it. That's all there is to it. She did it and you won't believe me."

That stupid condescending look again. God, he made me mad. Just when I was almost ready to begin the long forgiveness process.

"And she left with Gwen Schneider." No reaction. "The widow left my office with the mistress."

God, what was going to make a dent in that Herman Munster countenance of his?

I tried again. "Okay, listen. I get so violently dizzy around her that I sometimes pass out. Really. And you know I'm not a wimp, I'm not the fainting type. These feelings of mine are real. I guess I've never been around a murderer before, so this reaction is a lot more powerful than my usual ones."

"If that's the case, I understand you've been dizzy around O'Dear, too. So, if that's one of the criteria for being a murderer, it looks like he fits the bill also."

"Oh, don't be stupid." I dismissed his notion with a wave of a piece of bread. "Just arrest Carolyn and get it over with. Once you have her in your clutches, I know she'll tell you who her accomplice is. And it's not Michael O'Dear." I wouldn't admit to him that the same thought had been bugging me. Why was I off-balance around Michael so much of the time? It didn't make any sense to me. Just because he was the first guy I'd really fallen for since my divorce, that was no reason for me to be sick. Or was it? I was confused.

"I can't arrest someone on your hunches. Stay out of it. Let me do my work. If Carolyn Burns did it, then we'll find some evidence and arrest her. If she didn't do it, we'll find who did. You'll only get in the way. So please stop. Now, let's enjoy our meal and conversation."

Nice try. Thought he could pat me on the head and I'd shut up like a good little girl.

"Nope, your turn. You tell me what I want to know. This stuff is driving me up the wall. I know she did it, but I don't know how to prove it. Now you hold up your end of the deal. Spill it."

"Well, there's a few things I can tell you. Things that are pretty well known around here."

God, could he drag it out any more? "C'mon, tell me."

"Okay, but remember I'm only telling you this because it's common knowledge." He wiped up the final dregs of marinara sauce with bread.

Yawn. "Yeah, yeah, I know."

"Carolyn was not Burns' first wife." George took a second to lick his fingers clean and utter a contented sigh. "And Gwen was not Burns' first mistress. In fact, Carolyn was his first mistress when he was married to his first wife." A self-satisfied grin covered his face.

I needed a score card to keep up with this. "Burns apparently had an eye for the ladies. Who was his first wife? And where is she?"

"Her name is Claudia Wolfe Burns and oddly enough, she recently moved back to Quincy."

I know my eyes must have lit up. This woman was Carolyn's accomplice. It all fit. I just needed to meet her and to see how she "felt."

It all made sense now. Claudia was mad at Burns because of Carolyn. Carolyn was mad because of Gwen. And Gwen was probably mad because of the new one, whoever she was.

Claudia Wolfe Burns. That name sounded so familiar. I smacked myself on the head as it suddenly dawned on me that it was the name of the villain in *Bipolar Passion*, one of Carolyn's better books. Something didn't feel right about the scenario, but it did make sense. I needed to get more dirt from George.

George chuckled before I could ask him anything. "Why did you hit yourself in the head?"

I ignored his question and got to one of my own. "So,

why was Gwen released? Tell me the truth. Was it really because you heard her partial confession by eavesdropping, but you couldn't catch all of it?" Now it was my turn to chuckle. I could barely suppress my laughter, remembering how I'd caught him leaning against my office door.

"That's not important," he wiggled out of it. "But I do have some other stuff I can tell you."

"I'll be good, I promise."

He smiled again. "Apparently, some patients were going to sue Burns..."

I interrupted, "I know that. Michael told me."

"Yeah, but do you know why?"

"Maybe because files were lost or misplaced?"

I was just guessing, but it did make sense. It seemed unusual that Dr. Burns had a complete set of patient files in his office.

"Nope. This is pretty hush-hush so I don't know why I'm telling you..."

"Maybe you're captivated by my beauty," I joked.

He got serious. "Something like that."

For a moment he had an almost dreamy look in his eye but quickly shook it away. "Anyway a few patients thought that the descriptions in Felicia Greene's books struck pretty close to home. Some said they recognized themselves as characters."

"Wow, that makes sense. I saw Carolyn at the file cabinet. Did she steal the records?"

"Nothing was proven, and as of now people have withdrawn their suits since Burns' death. I'm going to be talking to them within the next few days though."

I couldn't hold myself back. Putting both my hands on his across the table, I said, "Please, please, please, let me go with you."

He merely shook his head. And didn't remove my hands.

"Okay, I understand you can't do that, but will you please tell me what they say? Please." I knew I was bordering on begging and that it was unattractive, but I was desperate.

"You know I can't promise to tell you anything else. Put the case aside and let's just relax and enjoy the rest of our evening." He adroitly changed the subject as I removed my hands. "Hey, I saw Cal the other day. He heard you were back in town and said to tell you hi."

Cal. Calvin Joseph Wade. B.H.'s partner in crime. His sidekick. His best friend in high school. Which meant he was our constant partner in double dating. And since he had the personality of a lizard and couldn't get up the nerve to ask anyone out, I always had to fix him up with my friends. After one date, they were no longer my friends.

"Ah, Cal. How is he?" Hopefully, George could tell that I really didn't want to know the answer to that question.

He didn't take the hint so we talked about how Cal was doing, and that led us into talking about old times again.

For a while I quit obsessing on the murder and enjoyed myself in spite of myself, surprising myself.

SIXTEEN

CLANCY AND I had just settled in for a good round of gossip when there was a loud knocking on the door. Again, I made the mistake of not looking before I opened it. I almost wished it had been the murderer.

In front of me was Georgianne, practically foaming at the mouth. She careened through the door before I had a chance to shut it in her face.

I forced myself to be cordial. After all, the house was in her name and I didn't want to be evicted.

She was not in the mood for friendly banter. "I am tired of people looking in your window all the time when you are gone. You promised me that there would be no further loitering and—."

"Lollygagging."

"Hmm?"

"I promised there would be no lollygagging. I don't think that loitering was ever mentioned."

She started pacing. "Don't you play games with me, young lady. There was a woman looking in your windows, and then another woman, then a man, and then another woman. Tell them to stop it. I cannot tolerate all of this stress. Having to look outside every time I hear a noise, it's hard on my nerves."

"How can I tell them to stop when I don't know who they are? Who are they, Georgianne?"

"I don't know, but make them stop. Your dog barks and I want to calm her down. She's a bit nicer than I thought." At that she stopped pacing and stooped to pet Clancy. "Gus says I can't just use our key anytime I think it's needed. But I told him I thought you'd want me to. So I came out to check on this darling dog and…By the way, don't you think 'Clancy' sounds rather common? She really looks more like a 'Fluffy' or a 'Princess' or perhaps…"

"Georgianne."

"Yes?" She didn't even have the good sense to look a little embarrassed.

"Focus. Tell me about the people who were looking into my house."

"Well, I didn't see them clearly because I don't like to pry. However, the first woman didn't look familiar to me at all. The second one looked remarkably like Carolyn Burns, although what she'd be doing here, I wouldn't even try to guess. Perhaps she's a bit miffed that you are spreading rumors about her being the murderer."

"Back on track, Georgianne. Who was the guy?"

"I'm sure I don't know, although he did look a bit like the one who was here the other night. Remember before the gas leak? And, Sam, Gus and I are so sorry about that leak. We were so sure everything was in tip-top shape back there. We feel just awful about your troubles."

"Awful enough to pay for my hospital bill? My insurance won't kick in for a month." I knew there was a chance it wasn't Gus and Georgianne's fault, that the murderer may have done it, but I couldn't help myself. Georgianne appears and I must say or do something to get her goat.

"Well, I'm sure something can be…now weren't we talking about those prowlers? Let's see the final one wasn't someone I'd seen often. But I think she was that Schneider woman."

Oh-oh, Georgianne looked like she was going to sit down and settle in. I had to stop her at all costs.

"Thanks for the information and I really appreciate your diligence in watching my place. Clancy, kiss Georgianne good-night."

What fun this was. I suppose I should've felt bad about the look of utter distaste and shock that covered Georgianne's face. But, nope, I reveled in it.

I didn't enjoy it however when Clancy kissed her and Georgianne absolutely swooned. I'd have to talk to Gus about what he was doing, or not doing, in the kissing department.

Georgianne got positively goo-goo-eyed over my dog. And it looked like my best friend was returning the favor. They were just lucky that I was too busy worrying about the prowlers and murderers to spend much time worrying about them. Clancy would hear about this treasonous behavior later.

I ushered Georgianne out of the door while listening to her "dear little doggie-woggie." I thought I was going to be sick. But this time I would know the cause.

I closed the door and locked it. "Clancy, I'll talk to you later about your unconscionable behavior. You ought to be ashamed. Right now I've got some important stuff to think about, so go to your room and I mean it."

Clancy went to her room and collapsed on our bed. Even though I couldn't see her, I knew exactly what she was doing. The dog version of "Camille." Dramatic. I'd make up with her later. She needed to feel the sting of my lack of affection for a while.

The parade that passed by my house this evening sounded like an interesting one. Who was the first woman? She must have been disguised or new in town for Georgianne not to identify her. Then Carolyn, Charlie, and Gwen. What a motley crew. I'd call Gwen tomorrow and find out why she was at my house. Carolyn's motive was easy to figure out. She was probably trying to decide how to kill me.

Okay, maybe I'm dramatic too. Anyway, Carolyn was up to no good. Of that I was very, very sure.

After I turned the lights off I noticed the insistent blinking of the red dot on the answering machine. I'd forgotten to check my messages. The first one was indeed B.H. saying that he would be late for dinner. So he hadn't lied after all, what a surprise. There was also one from Jen reminding me of her children's birthday party tomorrow evening. Both her kids were born on the same day, one year apart. It made planning parties quite easy for her.

I slept the sleep of the innocent and woke early enough for a wonderfully long walk. Clancy took this as a sign of amnesty and things were pretty well back to normal with the two of us. I did let her know how I felt about her attention to Georgianne.

"I don't know how you could be so loose with your affection. Remember that you pee on her plants because we don't like her. And you notice that it's *we* don't like her, not *I* don't like her." Then I resorted to a low blow. "Remember who feeds you."

Clancy glanced back at me from her vantage point at the end of the leash. She looked suitably contrite. I had no doubts, however, that she would lavish her fickle affection on Georgianne at the earliest available opportunity. Anything for a belly rub.

At home I toasted a bagel, gave a piece to Clancy and put peanut butter on my portion. As I chomped I looked around for something to wear to work. Vowing to give in and do some clothes shopping, I dragged out an old pair of khakis, prayed they'd still fit, and sucked in my gut as I struggled with the zipper. I paired the slacks with a big color-blocked sweater. It covered my hips and would be handy in case I split the seam on the pants.

Today was a great day to walk to work. I still didn't have my own car and also didn't have anything to carry to work except my purse. Clancy didn't whine when I said goodbye and I enjoyed the quick walk to the clinic. I wore sunglasses because the glare off the snow from the bright sun was blinding. No complaints though. The sight was mesmerizing.

Clara Schmitt was at her desk when I arrived. She handed a file to me. I actually had a second patient. I took a few minutes to read about Andy Duesterhaus, a thirteen-year-old boy who was described as sullen, moody, and non-communicative. Sounded like my kids when they were thirteen. He'd been referred by the school counselor and so far hadn't been seen by a mental health professional. I planned to do a diagnostic interview and formulate the diagnosis and treatment plan from there.

I had enough time to fill my coffee cup and take one sip when Clara announced that Andy was in the waiting room. Without being seen, I was able to peek around the corner to get a look at him. Andy appeared to be a normal, red-blooded American boy. He oozed contempt for grown-ups, had pierced ears, and his clothes looked like he had picked them out of a rag bin. I welcomed him, walked with him to my office, and offered him a seat. He didn't make eye contact but he sat.

"What brings you here today?"

The usual response from adolescents was something like, "My parents are raggin' on me. They think there's something wrong." Or, "Nothin'." Or even, "My parents made me come."

Andy's response was silence.

I tried a few more opening gambits. And got nothing from him. Not too unusual. The only noticeably odd thing about Andy was that he was clutching a laptop computer.

After talking for a few minutes with no response from the peanut gallery, I turned on the PC on my desk and began fiddling with it. He still didn't speak, but shortly the hairs on the back of my neck stood up because he was breathing on me.

"Way cool." Ah, he spoke.

"Pardon me?"

"Way cool. You're up to level four of *The Thundering Horde*. I've never seen an adult get past level two." I could feel his hands and arms moving behind me.

"I like computers and I like to play games." Not looking at him yet. Still playing the game. "What level you at?"

"I finished level ten, so I'm done."

"Cool. What else do you like to do?" Still playing my game.

"Playing *Sandblaster* is pretty fun and I kinda like that new game, *Aliens from the Deep*."

"I've never played those. Are they on your computer?" When he nodded, I asked, "Will you teach me how to play?"

I assumed his grunt meant "yes," so I continued. "Do you have those on your laptop or on a PC at home?"

He replied they were on both computers, then said, "Do you want me to show you now?"

Now it was my turn to nod.

He placed the laptop on my desk and turned it on.

I was a willing pupil. Andy was right, these games were fun, but a bit gory.

The "ding" signifying the end of the hour came all too soon, and I didn't feel a bit guilty about earning money for playing games. This was a good start to building a therapeutic relationship with Andy. Maybe next week, he'd even say hello before the computer got turned on.

I had no idea what was going on with him, but at least we were communicating. That was a start.

As I said goodbye to Andy in the lobby, my mind turned to my other task at hand. I needed proof that Carolyn killed her husband and also needed to find her accomplice. This Claudia Wolfe Burns appeared a likely candidate, but I couldn't imagine her—or anyone for that matter—teaming up with the snooty Carolyn Burns. Carolyn was not the type to have intimate female friends. She was too catty and was also the consummate flirt with men.

I also planned to figure out how the killer got out of the room without dragging blood along.

Before I left for the day I checked with Mrs. Schmitt regarding my schedule. I had three patients scheduled for tomorrow and three more for Friday. Things were looking up.

As I was getting my coat and locking my desk, I suddenly felt like going to Burns' office one more time. I left my things on my loveseat. The tape had been taken off Burns' office door and the police were finished with the room, but I still entered through the kitchen door. It was like my private entrance to the crime scene.

The room looked much the same. Someone had

cleaned off the fingerprint powder and the rug had been shampooed. Nothing was going to remove the blood though. I'd seen enough blood in my life, being from a large, rowdy family. The stain was now a dull rust color and formed a circular pattern around a lot of the room, with random splatters branching out. My bet was that the rug would be discarded in a few days.

I wondered who would make that decision. Heck, I didn't even know who my boss was yet. It was surprising how well the mental health portion of the clinic functioned without a doctor there.

The file cabinet beckoned me. I really didn't want to snoop, but it seemed a shame to pass up the opportunity to look in the drawer Carolyn had pilfered. Of course, I didn't have proof that she took anything, I just didn't buy her statement that she was looking for insurance papers.

This particular cabinet held patient files. Dr. Burns had copies of all the folders, even when others were the primary therapists. At first glance, everything appeared to be in order. Then I noticed Mrs. Abernathy's file was placed after a Jenny Agnew, when it should have been in front of it. There were several others out of place as well, as if they'd been filed haphazardly. I didn't know what to make of this, but filed the information in my brain—in the right order—for later retrieval.

Now seemed like a good time to read a few files. I'd already read Mrs. Abernathy's and even made a few notations myself in the clinic file near Clara Schmitt's desk. I noticed my new notes weren't copied into this file yet. I decided to look at other misfiled records. The first one after Mrs. Abernathy was Alonzo Baron. Then Clare Chaplin and Katrina Ditmeyer. I plucked them from the drawer and took them into my office.

No glaring errors or omissions popped out at me as I read. But some items in the patient histories seemed eerily familiar. I struggled with an ethical dilemma. It was wrong to take patient files out of the office or to make copies without the client's permission. However I really wanted to compare some of this information with Carolyn's books. If I could prove she used patient files as fodder for her books that would be one step closer to proving she was her husband's murderer.

I thought that I could scan a file and then email it to myself at home. Yet I didn't see that as being any better than making copies. Finally I compromised—I'd make copies of pertinent sections and then swore to myself I'd destroy them as soon as possible. The only other option was to bring Carolyn's novels into work with me and that would seem suspicious.

The copy machine jammed a few times. Of course. But I hurried and completed my task as quickly as I could. It was one thing being nosey, but it was quite another copying files illicitly.

As I returned the files to Burns' office, the matter of the blood spatters caught my attention again. How could someone have killed him and not be covered with blood? I remembered that the window had been open—an obvious entrance and exit, but that still didn't answer the blood question. There probably wasn't a clue to be found since the cops had gone over the room pretty thoroughly. I sat on the floor, right where Burns had fallen, and looked around. A picture of Gwen crouched in a fetal position behind the door flashed in my mind. Was it possible she'd been there the whole time? Nah, she didn't have any blood on her and besides, she wasn't guilty.

Time passed quickly as I lost myself in thoughts, but no solutions poked their heads through my reverie. It was already dark when I rejoined the present. I ran to my office and gathered my things, and practically ran home, hard to do in the dark and snow.

When I finally got home, Clancy got a hurried walk. I knew she was thinking that Georgianne was looking more and more attractive. "Clancy, this isn't a long enough walk, you're right, but I'm late for Rosie's and Annie's birthday party."

At that she stopped her baleful looks. Clancy loved my nieces and nephews, but I couldn't take her with me tonight since Jen's house would be full of people.

I arrived at Jen and Manh's house just as folks were sitting down to dinner.

"Aunt Sam."

"Aunt Sam, look over here."

"Aunt Sam."

"Come here, Aunt Sam. I want to show you something."

"Sit by me, Aunt Sam.

"Wahhhhh! I want Aunt Sam."

Murder, schmurder. *This* is what I really loved.

SEVENTEEN

ONE FAMILY TRADITION was for everyone to gather for all of the children's birthdays. Today Rosie and Annie were both celebrating. Rosie's real name was Hong, which translates to Rose in English, and Annie's Vietnamese name was Anh, which easily became Annie. They were on the threshold of teendom, but were still recognizable as human beings.

Since Rosie, at twelve, was the elder, she opened her presents first. Mine was no surprise. Money. It takes no thought or planning on my part, but it is also highly prized by the older kids. They especially like the note on the card.

"Oh, Aunt Sam. You didn't forget. 'Happy Birthday, Rosie. This is not underwear money. Have fun. Love, Aunt Sam.'"

Annie echoed her sister's emotions when it was her turn for presents. The kids all loved having so many cousins and aunts and uncles. That translated into lots of money and presents on the appropriate occasions.

I enjoyed being with my family. The noise and chaos spelled "home" to me. My mind kept drifting to the murder, however. I made sure I had some private time with Pete to let him know what I was up to.

Pete believed me when I said Carolyn was the culprit. He didn't question my gut feelings and he didn't make fun of my certainty. He did, however, make me promise to be careful and not to stick my nose in where it didn't belong. That wasn't a hard promise to make, since I was sure that my nose belonged right in the middle of this murder investigation.

The noise level increased as the kids got out different outfits to put on a dramatic performance. They'd been rehearsing for weeks. Annie put on her father's lab coat and glasses and Rosie pranced around in a discarded choir robe. Marty, one of Jill's sons, was adorable in a disposable surgical gown, mask, glasses, head covering, booties, and gloves. There was nothing of him showing, but I could imagine a contagious grin hidden under the mask. They were discussing ("we're not arguing, Aunt Sam") some of the intricacies of the performance, so I took the opportunity to get some work done.

I caught my sister's eye across the room. "Jen, I'm gonna use the phone. Can I go into your bedroom where it's quiet?"

I thought she said yes, but it was hard to tell above the

din. Anyway, her head bobbed a bit, so I took that as an affirmative.

My next task regarding the murder was to contact Claudia Wolfe Burns. I didn't know what kind of scam to use to get her to talk to me so I decided to try an unusual tactic, I'd tell her the truth.

I got the number from Information—for a fee—and she picked up on the second ring. "Hello."

"Hello, Mrs. Burns, this is Sam Darling."

"Good evening. What can I do for you?" Her voice sounded friendlier than Carolyn's.

"I'm employed at the clinic, Mrs. Burns, and—."

She interrupted with, "Please call me 'Claudia.'"

"Thank you, Claudia. I'd like to talk to you about your ex-husband's murder. When would it be convenient to meet?" I decided to give her no choice on whether we met or not, only when.

"I suppose I should be honest. I want to talk to you too. Would it be possible for you to visit my home this evening?"

Okay, I would have told the truth if I'd had a chance. Gee, this was going to be a cinch. I didn't really know exactly what I was going to talk to her about, but I still thought she might be Carolyn's accomplice. How would I bring that into a casual conversation?

It took about twenty minutes to enjoy the show and

twenty more to say goodbye to the whole clan.

Driving from Jenny's to Claudia's only took another ten minutes, but that was enough time for me to decide what I was going to do. I was going to tell Claudia my opinion of Carolyn's involvement in the murder. Then I was going to watch her face to see if she was surprised. If she stayed cool, then I might start talking accomplice theories. Otherwise I'd stay quiet about it. I'd play it by ear.

Also, I was going to monitor my sense of well-being. If I got dizzy, I'd know she was in on the murder.

She answered the door with a warm smile. It lit up her surprisingly unlined face. The smile was framed by dark hair with hints of silver. "Welcome." She motioned for me to take off my coat. "I hope it's all right for me to call you 'Sam.' May I get you some coffee or a cold drink?"

I declined. There was so much food in me from the party that I felt I could burst. But I didn't feel sick. Didn't feel much of anything. Maybe my vibes were taking a vacation or maybe the food had calmed them. Could she be the accomplice?

I followed her into a pleasantly furnished condo. Brand new. Paint smell still evident. I sat in an overstuffed chair while Claudia settled on the couch, pulling her legs under her as she nestled against some large pillows.

Deciding to cut to the chase, I said, "Why did you want to see me?"

She smiled. "You certainly don't mess around, do you?" Her smile faltered. "You said you wanted to see me first. What about?"

Suddenly it hit me. "Were you at my home last night?"

"Yes, I thought we could help each other."

Aha. The first prowler.

She continued. "I understand you think you know who killed Martin."

She was the only person who called Burns by his first name. "I'm quite positive I know one of the killers."

Eyebrows arched, she asked, "You think there's more than one?"

"Yes, I do. The killer I have in mind is not the type to slice Dr. Burns the way he was sliced. It was too messy for her to have done the actual deed."

"So you suspect Carolyn."

This was getting interesting. "Yes, what about you?"

"I think there's much more to Carolyn Burns than meets the eye. You might think that I'm just angry at being made a villain in one of her books, but that's not it. Or at least that's not all of it. Martin suspected that Carolyn was involved in some pilfering at the office. Not just recently either, mind you, but for the last several years."

"Pilfering what?"

She hesitated for a moment. "Some of Martin's staff reported patient case records were misfiled. And a few times there were some records missing. They were found later, though—in the file cabinet. It perplexed him."

Some new information, "I knew about the misfiling, but I didn't know records were missing. What did Dr. Burns think happened?"

"He was sure Carolyn used the files."

I pounced, "For what?" I needed corroboration for my theories.

"Carolyn used patient files to get ideas for her books."

"That's what I suspected too," I confided. "But why didn't Dr. Burns tell the police? It's definitely illegal to use that information."

"I don't know why." Her mouth drew down in a frown, pinching her brow together, forming a downward arrow on her forehead. It appeared she had a suspicion.

I decided to bypass grilling her on that matter, but would come back to it later.

"What's your interest in this? What do you have to gain if the killer gets found, whether or not it's Carolyn? You and Dr. Burns have been divorced for years."

She stood, walked around the coffee table, and sat on an ottoman at my feet. "I don't know you, but I need to talk to someone about this." I put on my most sympathetic face, dying to hear the scoop. She continued, "Have you heard that Martin had a girlfriend?"

"Yes, Gwen Schneider. Although she said they broke up and he was seeing someone else." The light bulb went on. "Was that you? Were you his new girlfriend?"

She looked unbearably sad and began crying. "Yes, when I moved back to Quincy we went to lunch to discuss some financial matters. One thing led to another and we realized we still had feelings for one another. I loved him. And I want to see whoever killed him get punished."

Did I believe her? Or was she trying to snow me? I wasn't getting any negative vibes from her. In fact no vibes at all. But there seemed to be congruency in what she said and the way she said it. I decided to take her at face value and trust that what she said was true. It seemed she had two major reasons not to murder Burns. One, she loved him and two, she probably received hefty alimony checks from him. If they just began seeing each other fairly recently, he probably didn't make provisions for her in his will. The will. That was something I needed to check out. I'd just bet that Carolyn was provided for handsomely in Burns' will.

Okay, back to Claudia. "Tell me more about Carolyn's using patient files. What made Dr. Burns suspect her?"

"He recognized some of his patients in the books."

"I was under the impression he didn't read her books. That he didn't quite approve."

She looked away. "Martin wasn't entirely supportive of Carolyn's career choice. That's why she used a pseudonym. For a long time he didn't even know she was published. He thought writing was a hobby and that's all. I don't know if he read the books. I just assumed he did because he told me he recognized some patients."

"Tell me more. Why would Carolyn continue taking files once she became good at writing?"

"She was making money with them. Big money." Claudia sat up straight and leaned forward as she looked me in the eyes. "Why should she have to be creative when it was all there, already invented? Every single book of hers had some of Martin's patients in it. She used them as protagonists, as villains, as bystanders. Remember *Bipolar Passion*, the one in which she villainized me? The whole book was based upon one of Martin's patients; he wouldn't tell me the patient's name because of confidentiality. But I bet you could find out. The same with *Anxieties Unlimited* and *Psychotic Mama*. She stole files, copied them, and used them for her books. Martin told me he confronted her and they had a horrible argument."

I wanted clarification. "When was the argument?"

The brow furrow appeared again. "I think it was the day before he died."

"During my interview, Dr. Burns received a phone call from someone. He said something like, 'Don't threaten me, I'll get it to you.' I wonder if that was Carolyn he was talking to."

"It could have been. Although I don't know anything about that phone call. I understand he was killed shortly after hiring you."

It all made sense. It all fit. Carolyn knew that Burns was going to expose her for the fraud that she was. With Burns dead, her source would dry up, but her royalties would not. At last I had a motive. Now, who was her accomplice?

She cleared her throat, and my thoughts returned to the present. "I said he was killed shortly after hiring you. That's right, isn't it?"

"Sorry, Claudia. I need to think a minute."

I really needed to address Michael. There was a good chance he could have helped Carolyn. But what was his motive? Love? Greed? Carolyn's hefty insurance payment was probably large enough for a 50-50 split to be satisfying.

Of course, I felt silly. I'd fallen for him and I didn't really know him. It was probably just a physical attraction on my part, but he'd also proven to be sweet and kind to me as well. He wasn't very amorous, but I suspected that was because he respected me or because I passed out on him, not because he was a slitter of throats. Well, I'd just have to talk to him and lay it on the line. Perhaps I could delay it a bit, however, until I'd nailed Carolyn.

Now that I knew her motive it was time to spring the trap. But how? They didn't teach us this in graduate school. I'd always been busy learning how to help people. Learning how to trap someone was a whole new ball game.

"Sam." Claudia interrupted my plotting. Her grief was evident. She must have really loved Martin Burns. "I don't know what to do with this information. I think I should tell the police, but I'm afraid I'll get in trouble because I didn't tell them earlier."

Synapses were firing all over the place in my cranium. "I understand your fear. Why don't you let me broach the subject with Detective Lansing? I'm a close friend of his, and I think I can keep you out of it. Okay?"

She was pathetically grateful. "Thank you. Thank you so much. Do you know that Martin talked to me about you?" My surprise must have shown. "Yes, he did. He called me right after hiring you. He thought you would be a fine addition to the staff. That was the last time I spoke to him. And it seems he was killed almost immediately after we said good-bye." Tears again.

I didn't know how I felt about an unpopular guy liking me, but I guessed it was better than the alternative.

Promising to stay in touch, I drove away, well below the speed limit for a change, and tried to sort all this out. Even though Carolyn's motive for murder was clear, I still believed she didn't commit the murder alone. She wouldn't want to get dirty and she also didn't appear to have a background in nursing or medicine. Maybe she knew how to slice a vein from writing her books, but I doubted it.

For the time being I decided to take Claudia at her word, that she was at home when Burns bit the dust. I had no reason to believe her, except that I experienced no twitches, pings, itches, or vertigo around her. I wondered if George knew that Claudia was Burns' new girlfriend. I hoped I was the one who would be able to tell him. Surprising him would be a treat.

Clancy was waiting for me. Even though it was getting late, I took her for a nice long walk, trying to put Burns and his murder out of my mind for the time being. I had jumped headfirst into this murder investigation. No looking before leaping for this gal.

The cold air cleared my head. "Clancy, you won't believe how cute the kids were tonight. You should have seen them all dressed up in their parents' clothes."

The idea hit me so hard I jerked to a stop. Therefore so did Clancy. "Omigod. They used disposable surgical clothing." I described how nothing of Marty showed when he was dressed in scrubs and accessories. I started walking again at a frenetic pace as I put the pieces together. "Those scrubs and glasses and booties are stored in the closet right outside Burns' office. No one keeps rigorous track of how many are used. No one would have noticed."

I slowed down as my lungs started to burn. "So they came in the window, and maybe hid somewhere, put on the scrubs and killed him. They could have put the scrubs in a trash bag and left the same way. If they looked anything like Marty there wouldn't have been any blood on them at all." I wanted to yell "Eureka" I was so proud of my discovery.

Then I thought about some of the other details. "Do you think George could be right? I mean about the gas leak and the car wreck being accidents."

She looked at me and I got her point. "Well, maybe I was driving a bit too fast for conditions. Hell, okay I probably was."

She smiled. "Yeah, you're right. My own cousin was the mechanic and even he said the brakes were shot. No one messed with them. And the carriage house is old, and so are the gas lines. So no one is after me."

Clancy looked relieved that I finally "got it."

"So then why did I get myself mixed up in this?" She shook her head.

Perhaps my family was right. Maybe I was nosy. Maybe I was co-dependent. Maybe I didn't want anyone to have fun without me.

Clancy and I returned home and she went to bed. Something was stirring in my brain cells and I decided to dig into Carolyn's books. I'd piled them next to the bed. I was embarrassed that I owned them all, because I didn't want people to know I read her kind of literature. And I used that term loosely. Carolyn's books were light, frothy, sexy, and at the same time full of psychological pathos. She was a bestselling author, and I was drawn to her books, even though I looked down my nose at them. I didn't claim to be consistent.

After hurriedly looking through her novels, I found my answer. I didn't even need the copied clinical notes I'd brought home from the office. I recognized Mrs. Abernathy in one of the books, thinly disguised as Mrs. Abercrombie, a lonely, bored, horny woman with erotic, neurotic dreams. Why hadn't I noticed this before? I turned to my canine co-sleuth, "I wish you could read. You could read the files while I checked the books."

More reading and cross-checking and the truth was evident. Anyone who had access to both the patient files and the books could see it.

I wanted to speak to Carolyn, but couldn't wait until tomorrow. Delayed gratification is not my cup of tea. "Clance, I gotta find out who helped Carolyn kill Burns. Do you have any ideas?" I was only half-kidding. If Clancy could talk, she'd probably tell me all the details of the murder, wrapped up in a bow.

It was too late to call anyone in my family for help. Most of them had little ones and they'd be in bed after the birthday party. The two unmarried ones, Rob and Pete, were both working late shifts again today.

Who could help me? I didn't want to ask Michael, as there was a possibility he was involved. That was a possibility I didn't want to consider, but it was there all the same. It was trying to stare me in the face, but I kept bobbing and weaving so it couldn't. I also didn't want to call George. This was something I wanted to do without official police involvement. Then, when I solved the case, George and my brothers would be more approving of my "meddlesome" behavior.

It was apparent to me that I could solve this and bring Carolyn to justice. I just needed an escort. Clancy could go with me, but she couldn't lend a hand if I needed one. She could lend a paw and a growl however, and that might come in handy. Who else could I ask? Suddenly the obvious answer appeared.

Gus. Gus could help me. Now all I had to do was to talk to him without Georgianne finding out. If I called, she would pick up the extension. It had happened before.

Maybe I'd just go over there and try to talk to Gus privately. It was late, but their lights were still on.

I approached their back door cautiously. "Gus." I whispered his name as I tapped on the door oh so lightly. My luck was not good.

"Sam, what are you doing out at this time of night?" Her curlers followed her voice and her scowl invaded the night.

"Georgianne, I'm sorry to bother you. Can I talk to Gus, please?"

"And your poor little doggy. She's had a busy day and should be getting her rest." Georgianne leaned down to pet Clancy, but this time Clancy was all business. She stood patiently and allowed the pat, but didn't roll over like the fickle companion she sometimes was.

I would not be sidetracked by Georgianne's attempts to win over my dog. "Can I talk to Gus, please?"

"He's not well." She stood up again; apparently convinced Clancy wasn't going to turn traitor. "Surely whatever it is can wait until tomorrow."

"This is important. Is Gus awake?"

Gus's booming voice cut through the gloom on the porch. "Sam, come on in, girl. What's up?"

As we entered the parlor, his wife looked at him with great concern. Even though I thought she was a real witch, it was obvious she loved her husband. She drove me crazy, but she loved one of my best friends. Guess I couldn't hate her as much as I wanted to. And now that she had a relationship with Clancy, it meant she loved two of my best friends.

Now it was time for me to test my courage. I looked Georgianne straight in the face and said, "Please let me talk to Gus alone. I promise it's important." She appeared to be softening. "Please, Georgianne. Please. It's important."

Without saying a word, she faded into the background. What luck.

Clancy and I waited patiently while she closed the parlor door and then turned to Gus, reclining on his usual sofa.

He sat at our approach. "What's up? What are you doing here at this time of night?" He patted the couch and both Clancy and I joined him.

"I really need your help. Remember how you told me that all this excitement is keeping you healthy and young?" He nodded. "Well, Gus, my friend, I've got something that'll probably make you feel like a teenager."

"I'm in. What are we going to do? Where we going?" There was no doubt why I loved this man.

"Okay, here it is. We're going to Carolyn's house. I want to see what's going on and maybe talk to her. I know why she killed her husband; now I just gotta figure out who helped her. You still willing to go?"

He grinned.

"And we're going to do it without the police."

My last sentence was lost on him, as he was halfway out of the door before I finished the question. I guess that meant "yes." We took my car.

EIGHTEEN

CLANCY JUMPED IN the back seat of the car, but managed to hang her head between Gus and me in the front. On the way to Carolyn's house, I filled in the blank spots for Gus. He already knew my suspicions about Carolyn, and he now knew the motive. I was getting nervous, and wanted a cigarette. I hadn't felt that way since the last time I'd had sex. It had been a while.

Gus didn't seem nervous, but his energy was at such a high level, I wanted to put him on a leash. I opened the window a crack to release a little of the heat. Soon, Clancy's head found the open window and behind my head I could hear her tongue flapping in the breeze.

When we arrived at Carolyn's house, I reminded Gus that all I really wanted to do was snoop around a little, and maybe talk to her. But that would depend on what we found out with our reconnaissance.

Carolyn's driveway held a car that looked vaguely familiar. I knew I'd seen it somewhere, but couldn't place it. I was relieved that it wasn't Michael's car.

As we would-be guerrillas stalked toward the house, I noticed a small figure peering furtively in the front window. This was interesting.

I turned to Gus and whispered, "I want to see who's looking in the window. I'm going to try to sneak up on her and see who it is. So just stay close by me. Close enough to help me, but far enough that you can get away if something happens to me. If she sees me, I'll just b.s. my way out of it. Keep Clancy with you." With a hand signal I motioned for Clancy to sit. I knew I sounded dramatic, but the situation didn't feel dangerous. "Don't worry, Gus. This feels real safe; just do what I asked, just in case I'm wrong. Okay?"

"Sure, but are you sure you don't want me to check this out? And you be the one who stays close by?"

I assured him that I knew what I was doing, surprising myself by my powers of persuasion. I almost convinced myself as well. Creeping forward, I felt like I was in a Grade B war movie. My adrenaline was pumping so drastically that my skin was on fire. It was almost like an energy field surrounded me. I heard Gus breathing close behind me. I trusted him. He would stick with me until the bitter end, but I sure hoped this end wouldn't be bitter.

Creeping closer to the prowler, I positioned myself directly behind her. "What are you doing?" It was difficult sounding commanding while whispering, but I think I pulled it off quite nicely.

The person whipped around—with a face that showed a state of fright that alarmed even me. "Charlie, what in the world are you doing here?" Finding scrawny Charlie Schneider peering in Carolyn's window surprised me.

"This lady in here is bad. I think she might hurt Gwen."

"Why do you think that she's going to hurt your sister?"

"Gwen's in there with her."

Oh, no. Gwen probably was here doing the same thing I was doing, trying to expose Carolyn and her accomplice. Why in the world would Gwen think she could handle this by herself? At least I had my trusty sidekicks, Gus and Clancy. And speaking of them, where were they?

No sooner had I thought the question than Gus bumped into me. I spoke quietly to him, "Do me a favor and take Charlie out to the car. Charlie, stay there and lock the door. Do not move. Will you do that?"

"I want to help Gwen."

I couldn't have Charlie trying to help. His behavior was unpredictable and I recalled the pistol brandishing of just a few nights ago. "Charlie, please go with Gus. Stay in the car and I promise I'll do what I can to keep Gwen safe. Clancy will stay with you."

Another thought came to me, "Charlie, do you have a weapon?"

He shook his head. "The cops took it at the hospital."

"Okay. Just stay in the car. I'll be right back."

Clancy did the predictable—tried to talk me out of being left behind, but I was able to convince her. "Please, I promise I won't have too much fun without you. Just stay with Charlie."

I assured Gus I'd wait for him to return.

Charlie and Clancy went with Gus, all three with feet dragging and heads hanging. I imagined it would take Gus a few minutes to settle Charlie down. It was hard waiting. I thought maybe I could just peek in a window while I was waiting for him to return.

I was even shorter than Charlie and couldn't see into the window. There was a wide ledge and I tried climbing up to peer inside. Perhaps I was a bit wider than Charlie was too, because I bumped against the window as I climbed into position. The "thud" was muffled, but it certainly echoed in my ears like a cannon. I convinced myself that no one heard it and proceeded to try to see something.

"Ms. Darling, perhaps you'd like to come inside to see what's happening in the house. It's much warmer and the view is better." Her voiced dripped with honeyed sarcasm. Even before I turned, I could picture Carolyn and imagined a gun in her hands.

I was wrong. She didn't have a weapon. In fact she looked weak and vulnerable. I knew better, but since I did want to go in her house, I took her up on her offer.

We walked inside. It was warm as she'd promised, but I still shivered. Even though Charlie said Gwen was here, there was no sign of her. "So, what are you doing sneaking around my home?"

"It's no secret that I know you killed your husband. Today I found out why. You took files from your husband's office and you used those files as plots for your trashy novels." So much for my plan to be discreet.

"I wouldn't call them trashy." She smiled. She must be nuts.

"You took the files, used them as plots, your husband found out and you killed him."

"Prove it."

"I recognized patients in several of your books, *Schizoid Revenge*, *Bipolar Passion*, *Farewell My Anxious One*. I also heard Dr. Burns talking on the phone right before he was killed. He said he'd have it for you soon. My guess is you found out about him and his new girlfriend and said you wouldn't divorce him unless he allowed you continued access to the files." This was pure speculation. I was making it up as I went along, but it looked like I'd guessed right.

"You certainly think you are brilliant, don't you? But your theories are ludicrous. Why would I kill him if I needed access to his files?"

Stumped me there. "Because you did, that's why."

In walked Gus, my superhero. "You okay, Sam?"

"Yeah, I'm fine. We need to call the police. I told Carolyn that I know everything now."

"Everything but who her accomplice is." The new voice entered the conversation with no warning. I spun around and saw—Gwen Schneider.

Gwen continued to stand there and grin. Her beautiful white teeth suddenly seemed predatory instead of just big and shiny.

My adrenaline no longer came from excitement, but rather from fear. I couldn't wait any longer. "Gus, hurry. Call George. Tell him that…"

As Gus dug for his phone, Gwen cut him off. "I wouldn't do that if I were you." The gun in her hand showed us she was serious, even though her dialogue was hackneyed.

"Gwen, what are you doing? You're innocent." My amazement was transparent. There was no way Gwen was holding a gun on my Gus.

Gwen and Carolyn looked at each other. They grinned and both grins morphed into almost maniacal laughs. Finally Gwen sauntered toward Carolyn and gave her a big kiss.

What? Had I fallen down the rabbit hole? Lewis Carroll said it right; this was getting curiouser and curiouser.

Carolyn sneered. "Close your mouth. It's most unattractive." I did.

Looking at Gus, I noticed that he didn't seem as surprised as I was. So Carolyn and Gwen were an item. Where were my vibes? Right in the pit of my stomach. I started feeling dizzy and ill. Surprisingly enough I didn't feel scared. I'd probably pay for that later.

I'd never seen them together before, but now that I did; I noticed my body working up into a tizzy. Gee, why couldn't I throw up on them? That would certainly distract them long enough for Gus at least to make his exit.

Gwen continued to stand with one arm entwined around Carolyn while her other arm supported the gun pointing at Gus. "Move over by your old friend." She motioned for me to get close to Gus. It was hard to walk as I felt I couldn't control my legs. But I moved. Suddenly her weapon covered us both.

Gwen said, *sotto voce*, "Now all we have to do is figure out how to get rid of them."

"Whoa, Gwen, I heard that. You don't have to get rid

of us. Tie us up here, and leave town. Leave the country. Leave the planet for all I care. Just leave and you won't have to do anything to hurt us."

Gwen sneered again. "This isn't the movies. You can't talk us into letting you go. This is real life and we want to stay here in Quincy." Her river rat accent reappeared. "You and Gus have got to be eliminated."

Okay, plan two. "How about letting Gus and me move out of town?"

"Shut up."

She was serious. All I could think about was that I needed to stall. As a crisis specialist I knew that the longer people go without using a weapon, the less likely they are to use it. I calmed enough to know it was time to chatter. "Hey you guys, I hate untidy endings, and you know I'm nosy. Before you kill us, will you just explain some things to me?"

Carolyn shook her head. "No, we are not going to explain anything to you. You're trying to stall and that's not going to work."

"Wait, honey," Gwen interrupted, "I'd love to fill the nosy little bitch in on our plans. It won't hurt anything and I'd like to let her know how wrong she's been all along. It's been such fun watching her foolish moves, trying to prove my innocence." Gwen motioned with her gun again. "Both of you sit on the love seat where I can watch you. And don't move a muscle."

It appeared to me that as long as we were sitting in Carolyn's living room we were pretty safe. Carolyn was much too fastidious to allow Gwen to make a mess here. It was also obvious to me that while Carolyn was mercenary and self-centered, Gwen was cold hearted and dangerous, the bloodthirsty leader. Of course, I'd been wrong about her before.

"What do you want to know?" Gwen looked like a cliché of a gangster in a movie from the 1930's. She curled her lip, gestured with her gun, and glared at me in a predatory manner.

"I've got lots of questions. First, which one of you did it and why?"

Before either of them could answer, I continued, "Oh God, now I see it. Gwen, when I found you on the floor in Burns' office, you hadn't just come in, had you? You were there already when Doris 'discovered' the body."

Her smile chilled me. "Go on."

"That's why you kept confessing to me. You thought I'd figure out that you'd been in the room the whole time and you were trying to convince me it was an accident. So the footprints outside the building must have been Carolyn's. Burns returned to his office after taking me to the personnel office. You two were waiting for him. Which one of you sliced him?"

Carolyn looked at her girlfriend. "If you want to talk about it, please hurry up. I want to get rid of them."

Gwen spoke to Carolyn but didn't take her eyes off us, "Don't worry. I'll hurry. I just want the satisfaction of looking at the stupid bitch's face when she realizes how we've made a fool of her."

I thought they didn't have to make a fool of me. I'd already done quite nicely on my own.

I wanted to keep Gwen talking. She'd gone over the edge and my best bet was to encourage her bragging. "So Carolyn told Burns she'd give him his freedom if he'd give her continued access to the files. He refused. So you cut him. And after you killed him, you helped Carolyn back out the window. You probably didn't count on Doris coming into Burns' office. When she walked in, you slid to the floor behind the door and stayed quiet until the room filled up with the rest of us."

"About time you figured it all out. How we laughed at you and your amateur sleuthing. We realized pretty early you were no threat to us at all. You were just playing at crime solving. The only thing you were good at was bungling."

I let the jibe go unanswered. "I also want to know if either one of you sabotaged the gas line to my house or the brakes on my car."

"Of course not." It was Carolyn's turn to talk. "We

just saw those as signs that luck was with us."

I sensed they were starting to get bored with my questions, so I decided to throw them an interesting one. "What I really want to know is how you two got together. Carolyn, I know you were Dr. Burns' sweetie while he was married to Claudia. He divorced her, married you and then started a long-term affair with Gwen. So how did you guys get so chummy?"

"I think that's a fair question." Gwen turned to Carolyn. "Do you want to answer it or shall I?"

Carolyn did not seem pleased by the whole conversation. Of course she wasn't the center of attention and she didn't like that. "You tell them if you want to. I think we need to end the conversation and get on with ending their existence. I'm bored with all the talk."

Gwen faced us again. "When Martin ended our relationship, I was mad. Really mad. I wanted to kill the little chippie he was sleeping with. But he was so discreet. I couldn't figure out who it was. Then I got mad at him instead. For dropping me and then for being so sneaky that I couldn't figure out who he was seeing. I thought Carolyn might know something. I called her and told her Martin was having an affair with someone that wasn't me. We met. We talked. The rest, as they say, is history." God, she was unattractive as a braggart.

"I have another question. Did you ever find out who

Martin's new girlfriend was?"

Gwen didn't look so confident now. "No, but it doesn't matter. She doesn't have him any more."

Now it was my turn to gloat. I knew something they didn't know. Maybe I could use that as a bartering tool later.

"Okay, I have another question." Oops, I better make this interesting. Gwen and Carolyn were both starting to fidget. "Carolyn, did you send Gwen into my office to keep me busy while you were rifling through Martin's files? That was a good move and it almost worked." She nodded, she liked compliments. "The thing that made the plan fail was that Gwen kept looking at the door leading toward the kitchen. I knew something was going on so I walked through the kitchen and caught you in Martin's office."

Gwen wasn't happy by this turn of events. "Shut up, loser. Do you want to know anything else or are you ready to die?"

Okay, here goes nothing. "The other night there was quite a parade by my house. Would you explain that?"

Gwen giggled.

Carolyn's turn to talk, apparently. "It was quite a coincidence that we were both there. In fact we just discovered it today. You know Claudia Burns just returned to Quincy. I don't trust her and thought I'd check her out. As I was driving to her house I noticed she was leaving and I followed her. She went to your home, knocked, and peeked in the window. Don't know why. As she left, I looked in your windows."

Carolyn continued. "Gwen's brother Charlie has this thing about trying to protect Gwen. He was following me, because he thought I was out to hurt Gwen." She flashed a loving smile at Gwen. "Gwen was out looking for Charlie because she wanted to tell him about our relationship so he would stop worrying and would stop snooping. That's how we all ended up looking in your windows within a very short time. Rather funny when you think about it."

"Yeah, it really tickles me." God, I hate it when I resort to sarcasm.

Carolyn's recent and short bout of good humor left her. "Gwen, we've talked long enough. Let's get out of here. We can get down to the river and kill them there. There are so many sink holes that we can load them down with bricks after they are dead and just let them sink. No cleaning up to do. And there are probably plenty of bodies down there to keep them company." Just when I thought Carolyn was the saner of the two, she went and got weird on me.

"Okay, but please," I pleaded, "please answer one more question..." They stopped walking so I continued with a question I already knew the answer to. "The thing that's driving me crazy is how did you clean up after the murder?" Looking at Gwen, I said, "There was no blood on you anywhere."

Since I sounded as if I admired their brilliance, Gwen couldn't stop from answering. "You are such a dope. Clinics are full of disposable gowns. After Martin refused to cooperate, Carolyn kept talking to him while I stepped into the closet outside his office, got some gowns, gloves, hair coverings, and booties. I looked into Martin's office, asked him to excuse us for a moment, and called Carolyn into the hallway. We went into the kitchen, covered ourselves with the disposable stuff and went into Martin's office through that door."

"Wasn't he surprised to see you both dressed like that?"

She continued, "I don't think he knew who we were right away. By the time he figured it out, it was too late."

"So you actually cut him? You're the one?"

She didn't speak but she grinned, and that gave me all the answer I needed.

I continued with my questioning. "Then you put all the disposable clothing and the scalpel in a plastic bag and helped Carolyn out of the window. She took the bag with her. That's why there were footprints leading away from but not toward the building."

"Bingo," Gwen said, "you win the door prize." She paused. "Too bad there isn't one." Again, the maniacal laughter.

It caused my spine to shiver uncontrollably.

When she stopped laughing she said, "I was the receptionist, so I was the only one who knew Carolyn had come into the clinic. She'd called him from the empty office—now it's yours—and when he got nasty on the phone we just decided to get rid of him. We figured I'd still be working there and could give new files to Carolyn. Of course, things didn't quite work out the way we'd planned."

Carolyn couldn't resist trying to stop the chatter. After all, the attention wasn't focused on her. "Will you just get rid of the bitch and the old man? You've told them everything. Sam's just stalling."

Gwen agreed to stop talking and bragging and to get the job done. "Get up. Get up. Let's go." The way she brandished that pistol, I was scared I'd die accidentally. She didn't appear to have any more expertise than Charlie did. Maybe I could get the jump on her. I thought that if there was some way I could signal Gus, or some way to let him know that he needed to deal with Carolyn, we had a chance. Carolyn was a wimp. Gwen wasn't, but we had to do something. I wasn't going to die without at least mussing up someone's hair. And if I was going to die, I wanted it to be here, so I could bleed all over Carolyn's beautiful carpet. I decided to be resolute and just go for it.

As Gus and I stood, I melodramatically clutched at my stomach and yelled, "Grab Carolyn."

Luckily Gus didn't second-guess me. He jumped up and literally threw himself at Carolyn, tackling her in a way that showed her he knew his way around a football field. At the same time I pretended to pass out on Gwen. It wasn't as picture perfect as Gus's execution, but it was dramatic and it worked. My reputation as a fainter preceded me. She dropped her gun as the nurse in her reflexively put her arms out to catch me. I immediately grabbed Gwen and put her in a basket hold—a restraint normally used only for my past psychiatric patients and younger brothers. Expertly executed and very effective.

Just as I wondered how long I could hold her, we were pleasantly interrupted. "Hold it right there. Don't move." George's voice was beautiful at that moment. I swirled around to face him and instead saw not only George, but Michael, Pete, Rob, Georgianne, and a charging Clancy. Georgianne was replete with the ubiquitous housecoat and curlers.

I maintained the restraint hold on Gwen, but I was getting tired. Clancy revealed teeth I didn't know she had as she growled at Gwen, letting her know her bite was definitely going to be worse than her bark.

"Will someone help me here?" I yelled. Rob rushed over and relieved me of my charge.

Gus left Carolyn on the floor and went to his bride. "Darlin', I don't think I've ever seen you look so lovely." I swear to God she blushed. And she almost looked good. Hell, she did look good. Anybody who helped saved my life was beautiful.

George took charge. "Rob, Officer Radcliffe should be coming inside any minute. Read these two their rights and take them downtown. I'll be down in a little while to question them."

He looked at me. I couldn't help myself. I hugged him. Then I hugged Michael, and Pete, and Georgianne. I got on my knees and kissed my brave dog. I promised Rob a hug later, as I didn't think he'd appreciate being grabbed by his big sister as he was arresting two murderers.

On her way out the door Carolyn looked seductively at Michael in one last-ditch attempt to garner his support. Michael didn't make eye contact with her.

I stood and faced George. "Where's Charlie?" The last I knew, he was in my car with Clancy?"

"Another officer is speaking to him outside. Are you okay?"

I didn't answer; instead I asked another question.

"How did you find out we were here?"

"It was Georgianne. She knew where you and Gus were going and she called me. I came right over and was rather surprised to see the rest of this gang here as well."

I looked at the beaming Georgianne. "How did you know we were here?"

"Well, you know Gus isn't well. I think it's my job as his loving wife to know his whereabouts at all times. So I listened when you were talking to him. And don't you dare call it 'eavesdropping.' I was doing it for Gus's own good, and for yours too as it turned out."

How could I be mad at the beautiful old witch? She saved us. "And what about my brothers?"

"Well, you told me your brother Rob is a police officer, so I called him, thinking that Officer Lansing could probably use a little help. And I remembered that your brother Pete is a Father, so I called him. You never know when you might need a priest. It just so happened that both young men were arriving home from work when I called and they were most happy to hear from me."

I felt Rob's stare as he and Radcliffe led the duo away. "We're going to have a nice long talk later about your midnight activities," he said.

I bet he wanted to thank me.

Pete contributed his unwelcome thoughts. "What in

the hell did you think you were doing?"

"Pete, priests shouldn't cuss."

"Stay on the subject. What did you think you were doing?"

"Well, Father Smarty-Priest, I thought I was doing exactly what I did. Gus and I solved the crime and we caught the criminals. If I hadn't pretended to faint on Gwen, she would have killed us and if Gus hadn't tackled Carolyn, why she might have..."

"If you hadn't come snooping around, you wouldn't have been in a position where you had to be theatrical to save yourself."

Male logic. Can't live with them. Period.

George hung up the telephone, where he'd been talking with the station. "Pete, will you do me a favor and give Mr. and Mrs. Granville a ride home? They look tired. I'll take Sam home in a few minutes."

Georgianne and Gus looked anything but tired. Georgianne was still glowing and Gus had the energy of a thirty-year-old. Romance was in the air tonight.

Both of them hugged me before they were escorted from the room. As he was walking out, Gus turned to me and said, "This was the best night of my life. Thanks."

The room emptied out pretty quickly. I was left with George and Michael. Michael hadn't yet spoken to me, although I could feel his eyes on me the entire time. It was time for me to hug him again. My vertigo was settling down. Maybe I was "vibed out" for the night. I now knew that Michael had nothing to do with the murder. Why did I feel dizzy around him and not around Gwen? She was one of the guilty ones.

I walked up to Michael, put my arms around him and suddenly knew. I whispered in his ear "Maybe you scare me." That's the only reason I could think of for my physical reaction to him. "Maybe you scare me, Michael."

"And maybe I should," he whispered back. His warm breath in my ear caused shivers and goosebumps, but no dizziness.

George interrupted again. "I want to give you a ride home, because I need to talk to you. O'Dear, will you follow me in Sam's car? Then I'll give you a ride back here to your car?"

Michael was much too agreeable. He said yes and took Clancy with him. George and I got into the unmarked cop car that everyone in town recognized.

The ride was only a few blocks. I sat with my head leaning back, thinking about tonight, what almost happened, and what did happen.

"Hey." He startled me a bit.

"Yeah, what?" My words were said quietly.

"First of all, I'd like to call a truce. I'm sorry about the prom. That was a long time ago and I hope you can start treating me like a human being again. I'd like to be friends."

I was feeling magnanimous. Surviving a near death experience tends to bring out the best in me. I turned to him and smiled. "Okay. I'm willing to forgive and forget."

And then he did the strangest thing. He put on the brakes, leaned over and kissed me.

And I did the strangest thing. I liked it.

This was crazy. Crazy. Michael was the guy for me, not balding old comfortable George.

"That's the way I like you, Sam. Quiet." He laughed and eased the car back into gear again.

Not only was this crazy, but Michael was behind us. I wondered if he saw anything. Oh, God, that would be awful.

We arrived at my house without us exchanging another word. I stayed in the cop car, in a semi-daze, as George got out and opened the passenger door for me. I exited slowly. Michael got out of my car, walked up to me, and handed me my keys. They each took an arm and escorted me to my front door. I was in awe of this situation. Over the past few years, I had become a Dateless Wonder. Suddenly there were two guys interested in me.

I opened my door and Clancy ran inside. I turned and

without speaking watched Michael and George walk off into the sunrise together. Okay, it was a street light, but it had the same effect. Not exactly the ending I would have planned for this adventure.

I'd probably see them both tomorrow. That would be fun. And I'd see them at the trial. That would be even more fun, because I'd get credit for solving the case. For now I needed to prepare myself for the inevitable letdown that comes after an adrenaline-laced crisis.

So I wasn't a superhero. Some might say I wasn't a hero at all. But I did solve the murder. Well, I was wrong for a while, and I was wrong about a couple of the participants, but I did solve it. That felt good. I mentally ran down the list of siblings that I needed to call in the morning and brag to.

Hard to believe that less than a week ago I was unemployed. Now, I was employed and was a hero. The only negative spin I could put on this thing was that I left the adventure the same way I entered it—with my virtue intact.

Again, not the ending I'd envisioned.

I looked at my faithful companion. "C'mon, Clancy, let's go for a walk. We've got a lot to talk about."

She smiled.

Want more? Buy the second Sam Darling mystery, "Any Meat in That Soup?" right now. Or for an even better deal, buy the box set of the first three books, "Triple Trouble!"

Read on for the first chapter of the next book…

About
ANY MEAT IN THAT SOUP?
(Sam Darling mystery #2)

When a man falls down at Samantha Darling's feet, she thinks it's pretty funny. But she stops joking when he turns up dead.

Social worker and would-be crime-solver Sam is busy trying to unravel the mystery as the death toll keeps mounting. She's thrilled to be hired by the handsome local private eye to work in the ER and investigate, but her elation quickly evaporates when she finds out that her sister Jen is being investigated for the murders.

A trio of other suspects, a poisoning scare for her best bud and canine companion Clancy, and the back-and-forth pull of Sam's attraction to the dreamy Michael and the loyal George keep her unbalanced as she tries to juggle social work, secret sleuthing, and a romantic triangle.

As usual, Sam takes her snooping to extraordinary heights. She can't seem to stop putting her nose where it doesn't belong. And this time...she may have gone too far.

CHAPTER ONE
Any Meat in That Soup?
(Sam Darling mystery #2)

He fell at my feet. Nice place for a man. Problem was, he was blue. Maybe dead.

It seemed like an eternity before a sea of color descended on him. One white coat checked for a pulse. A Mickey Mouse scrub suit listened for breath sounds. Someone in jeans and a sweater retrieved a gurney. Mickey Mouse put a finger in the man's mouth, and swept it from side to side, looking for God-knows-what.

A green scrub suit said, "On my mark. One, two, three." The sturdy group of four lifted my dinner companion and placed him on the stretcher.

My sister, Jenny—the guest of honor at this birthday party—orchestrated the procedure. As the nurse manager of the Emergency Department, she couldn't enjoy the festivities while there were chests to be pounded.

My other sister, Jill—she was the one in jeans and sweater—joined her. Even though Jill was off duty today, she was an ER resident and couldn't bear to sit and watch.

"Damn, Sam, when we tell ya to knock 'em dead, we don't expect you to take it literally."

"Shut up, Rob." I said to my brother, the smart-ass cop. "He's not dead. I saw him breathing."

He grinned. He knew how to push my buttons. Too bad he was such a little cutie; I found it hard to stay mad at him.

After the hubbub subsided, the rest of us returned to the mundane task at hand. Eating the goodies.

A visitor might remark that we were eating in the midst of a crisis. Any one of us would reply, "Yeah. And…?" Crises were something we were used to.

I looked around. My brothers were being their usual selves, joking with each other and happily munching on chicken wings. Other Emergency Department employees and guests relaxed in the staff lounge as they also enjoyed the food. The small dark room was made more festive with Happy Birthday signs and crepe paper throughout. Danny Jacobsen and Connie Mumford were having a heated discussion about the importance of exercise to maintain good health, as Danny ate a pulled pork sandwich and Connie started on her second. As a paramedic and nurse respectively, their experience, both in the ER and with carry-ins, kept them calm during the crisis.

"Hey, you two. For a married couple, you sure argue a lot." They both turned to look at me. "But it sounds like you were arguing the same point." I smiled as I said it.

Connie replied, “We do that all the time. We think we’re disagreeing and then notice that we’re on the same side. Crazy.” She looked at Danny, her bright brown eyes practically disappearing because of her huge smile.

Danny didn’t say anything. Just grinned. He was a man of few words unless he was arguing with Connie.

I noticed a pale, thin guy sitting by himself in a corner. He wore a white shirt and pants, and it was hard to see where his skin ended and the fabric began. The guy would take a bite of food, and as he chewed, he kept looking from side to side and over his shoulder. He was attached to the corner and was mostly in shadow, so it wasn’t easy to see him. I moved closer to Connie and asked, “Who’s he?”

Connie replied, “Oh, that’s Carter. He was just laid off as an EMT, but he still stops by here every day.”

“I’m not one for talking about people,” I fibbed, “but he looks creepy.

“I agree,” she said, “but he worked here for several years. He’s harmless.”

At that point Jill returned, blonde ponytail pleasantly mussed, a confused look on her face.

“Who took my plate?”

“No one,” I replied. “It’s right where you left it. How’s my date?” I took another slurp of the vegetarian vegetable soup, which was almost the only thing in that room that didn't stink of burnt flesh.

Jill's brow furrowed, then relaxed again. "First of all, he's not your date..."

I interrupted with, "Were we, or were we not, dining together?" Silence. "I think that constitutes a date."

Jill ignored me as she started munching on the Buffalo wings again. "And secondly, he'll be fine. We don't know exactly what it is yet, but it doesn't look serious. Heart looks okay, but his pulse is elevated, blood pressure is low, and he's dehydrated. Smelled like alcohol. How lucky could someone get...passing out in an emergency room." She smiled between bites. "They're admitting him to run some tests. Dougie's on duty."

Dougie was Dr. Kareem Douglas Johnson. Short, dark and handsome. And young. A resident in the ER where his mom, Loretta, worked as a technician. He was a rising star, so I had no doubt he'd take good care of..."Hey, what's the guy's name anyway?"

Jill shook her head as she munched on another bite. "Dunno. He's a homeless guy. One of our regulars. Says his name is 'Pluto,' so that's what we call him. He was hanging around outside, so I invited him to join us for Jenny's party. Gave him my plate and made another." She smiled. "Looks like he wasn't a vegetarian. He sure ate a lot of those wings before he keeled over."

I looked at Rob again. "Can't you quit licking your

lips over those chicken wings? It's practically making me ill."

He made even more noise. "Just because you're a vegetarian doesn't mean that we carnivorous types can't enjoy eating flesh." He licked his lips again, but this time widened his eyes and chuckled a la Hannibal Lector.

"One of these days you'll see I'm right. It's a well know fact that people who eat meat get sick a lot more than vegetarians. And besides…"

Rob interrupted with a rather loud belch. "I don't feel so good."

I looked skyward and mouthed a silent, "Thank you, God," but my sick sibling didn't notice.

Jill quickly became a doctor again. "You want me to look you over?"

"Nope, think I'll go home. Probably got a touch of the flu. I'll be fine." I knew Rob must feel really bad, because he didn't make a wisecrack.

He exited, looking slightly green and holding his stomach.

I turned to Jill. "That sure happened fast. What do you think it is?"

"Probably just the flu. Lots of it going around. The ER's been full of people who think they're dying, but just have a stomach virus. Not much we can do for it. We just tell them to stay in bed, drink lots of fluids and to eat when they can."

"Yeah, but they don't seem to think that's enough," Jenny chimed in as she reclaimed her plate. "They're feeling so rotten that they want antibiotics at the very least. And they're disappointed when we say they need to rest and drink a lot of fluids." She took another big chomp out of a chicken wing. "Gosh, most people left before we cut the cake. You guys want some?"

"Yeah, as long as there's no meat in it." They laughed at me but I didn't react. Hell, the intense smell of chicken, pork, and beef in that small room was so overpowering it nearly grossed me out. But not enough to stop me from eating other stuff.

As Jen handed slices of cake to Jill and me, I asked again about Pluto. "So is the guy going to be okay?"

"Don't know. I was going to wait a while and then call upstairs to check. If you have a few minutes, I'll call now."

I nodded, my mouth too full of cake to talk.

By this time the room had cleared except for Jill and me. Our other brothers left soon after Rob did, but not before making fun of him for taking off sick. Jill and I sat in companionable silence. Munching.

Jen returned, minus the grin. "Nurse in ICU told me that Pluto died just a few minutes after he was admitted."

"What happened?" Jill looked up expectantly.

"Don't know for sure. They might do an autopsy to find out what happened, but the nurse I talked to said he smelled like alcohol, so maybe that had something to do with it. Dougie'll be down in a minute or so and we can ask him."

"I don't remember him smelling like booze when he was sitting by me, but the smell of this barbecued meat kind of kills my ability to smell anything else."

"'Shup' about the meat." Jen was the sibling closest to me in age. A year younger and normally a lot nicer than I was. Yet I wasn't surprised at her "shut up." The gang got tired of my carnivore comments.

I decided to ignore her retort. "Will the cops have to come to check out Pluto's death?"

Jill and Jen both started talking at the same time, "Probably not." "Maybe."

They looked at each other and laughed. Jill continued, "It's hard to say. This death will probably fall into the gray area. Since there was no sign of physical injury and no obvious cause of death, the police might feel they need to check it out. But we have lots of deaths that fall in the gray area, and they aren't always investigated. Too bad Rob went home sick. He could've saved some other cop a trip."

Our youngest brother Rob was a rookie police officer in our hometown. He wore the "QPD" patch proudly.

The Quincy Police Department was small but pretty efficient, so I expected someone to show up momentarily.

"Hi ya, Sam." The new arrival was right on cue.

I cringed. It was George Lansing, my old, unlamented boyfriend from high school, dressed in his usual Detective Colombo-like rumpled suit.

"Hi, George."

Jen and Jill chimed in with "Hi, George."

My feelings toward George were ambivalent. He abandoned me on prom night twenty-five years ago. I've been told I hold a grudge. The jury's still out on that as far as I'm concerned.

After gracing me with his infuriating smile, he turned to Jill and said, "Jill, I was walking through the ER lobby when I heard that there was a sudden death with no known cause. Do you know anything about it?"

She nodded, "His name was Pluto, a homeless regular here in E.R. We had a little birthday party for Jen…"

"Happy birthday, Jen."

Jenny smiled and nodded her thanks.

Jill continued, "…and while he was eating, he passed out at Sam's feet."

A sound escaped from George that sounded like a snort of laughter. I glared, but he ignored me.

"What happened then?"

"We did some preliminary work on him here, but

then rushed him up to ICU after we temporarily stabilized him," Jill said. "That's really all I know. It didn't look too serious from what I saw. I'm pretty confident it wasn't a heart attack from what they said…but Dougie was the doctor in charge and it was his call. I just phoned ICU a few minutes ago and they told me he died."

George took notes as Jill talked. He looked up, "I don't really know yet if we'll be investigating. We'll probably wait until after an autopsy, if they do one. But if you guys don't mind, I'll want to talk to you three individually. Just in case." He paused, then added, "And do me a favor, tell Dougie—what's his full name?"

Jill answered, "Johnson. Kareem Douglas Johnson. He's a new resident in E.R. I think you know his mom, Loretta. She's been a tech here for a long time."

"Thanks for the info. Tell him I may want to see him in a few minutes. As I said, I don't know if we'll launch an investigation until after the autopsy. Will the three of you wait for me here while I go upstairs and check things out? I'll let you know then if I want to interview you or not."

Jenny and Jill both answered in the affirmative. I did not.

"Sorry, George. I have a date tonight. With Michael. Michael O'Dear. You know, the private eye?"

"Of course, I know O'Dear. We worked together on the Burns' murder...Hell, Sam, you know that. You were there. Trying to impress me that you have a date?" His words sounded mad, but his smile said something different.

"'Course not. Just wanted you to know I can't wait all night for you."

He waited for the inevitable.

I didn't give in.

He finished for me, "You mean you won't wait for me like you did on prom night."

I ignored the comment. "Is it okay if I go? I can talk to you tomorrow."

"Yeah, come down to the station." He turned away, then back again, continuing with his Columbo imitation. "Unless you want to meet me for breakfast?"

"Sure. Seven o'clock at The Dairy?"

He grunted and began walking toward the elevator.

"And, George?"

Another grunt as he turned to face me again.

"Don't stand me up."

I swear the final grunt had a smile in it.

Don't miss the third book in the Sam Darling mystery series, "Can You Picture This?" or get the bargain price and buy three books at once! "Triple Trouble" includes the first three books in the series.

"Will You Marry Me?," the fourth Sam Darling mystery, has also been released, and "Where is Henderson?" will be available by the end of 2014. Read on for how to contact the author and join her mailing list so that you'll hear about each new book right away.

ACKNOWLEDGMENTS

I'm grateful to so many people who helped birth this book. My first thanks go to Patrice Fitzgerald, of eFitzgerald Publishing, who is not only my publisher but my friend. Early on when I needed encouragement there were several people who filled the bill—Authors Beth Amos, Nelson Thurman, Cyndy Mobley, Lynnette Spratley, Debbie Puente, and the late Charlie Alexander. Thanks also go to editor Diana Kohn; agent extraordinaire, the late Jim Cypher; and producer Tim Grundmann for their help with the early stages of the manuscript.

Encouragement also came from my writers' groups over the years: the Aspiring Writers' Club, Housewife Writers, Easy Sisters, and ComedySportz Writing Group. Finally, I want to thank my final "first readers," Jan Bozarth Smith and Nikki Shields, who renewed my enthusiasm for my book.

A special thanks is due to Toni Taylor from Tiger Imagery who allowed us to use her lovely photograph as a basis for the cover. The house represents the home of Gus and Georgianne Granville in the book. Thanks as well to Jason Anderson of Polgarus Studio in Australia for speedy and reliable formatting.

Although people in Quincy, IL may recognize some of the buildings of our town, they won't recognize any of the inhabitants, because they existed only in my imagination. I do hope you see the love I feel for Quincy and understand the reasons I moved back home.

Best-selling author Jerilyn Bozarth Dufresne is the oldest in a family of nine children, which is where she got the inspiration for the Darling Family—although her sibs fight a lot more and have cornered the market on sarcasm. She returned to her hometown of Quincy, Illinois after having lived a nomadic life in her middle years.

Jerilyn currently works as an outpatient therapist at a local mental health clinic and teaches at Quincy University. She and her dog Gus live with, and are tolerated by, two cats.

To hear first about new books by Jerilyn, sign up at http://eepurl.com/z30jv . Your email will never be made public and you can opt out at any time.

Made in the USA
Lexington, KY
06 September 2019